I0653583

Ximena

Future Fiction London

XIMENA
By Hillary Raphael
Published 2008 by Future Fiction London
www.futurefiction.co.uk
ISBN 978-0-6152-0813-8
Copyright ©2008 by Hillary Raphael
All world rights reserved
Cover design by Gilded Peony
Cover photograph ©2007 by Crazy Beast

Special thanks to the Library of Congress Hispanic Division.

To Theodore and DSB.

Ximena

Future Fiction London

You, Luz-divina, must, by now, reside in hell.

You tormented me, humiliated me, robbed me of my joy of humiliation and my delight in torment, sapped my faith in the basic purity of humanity, and forced me to sell the one good tapestry in my collection. May your divine light glow sickly hot and carcinogenic green in your cold Bronx sepulcher. The modest burial the State has magnanimously provided, spreading smugly the largesse of the taxpayers who never even knew you (and from whom you stole honest employment), was lavish in comparison to what you deserved. They ought to have run your remains through a blender and fed them to Segismundo, saving just a few brittle crystals to salt the rim of my margarita glass, but right…they don't serve tequila cocktails in Ladies' Prison, not even to model prison librarians. No, more than a model prison librarian, I'm a supermodel prison librarian, but still: no frosty drink for me, Margarita.

My Personals at the time of this writing:

- 15 fl. oz. pump bottle of Baby Magic baby bath
- 16 fl. oz. screw top bottle of Woolite fabric wash
- genuine Birkin bag, chocolate "elephant skin" embossed calfskin
- YSL Rouge Pur lipstick #82
- green leather Swedish clogs
- Calderón de la Barca, Pedro. *Life Is a Dream/ La Vida es Sueño: A Dual-Language Book.* Ed. Stanley Appelbaum. New York: Dover Publications. 2002.
- Tinactin spray powder for feet
- 3" x 5" photograph of Segismundo in silver-plated frame
- magnetic locker mirror
- unlined writing paper and cheap ballpoint pen
- enteric-coated Acidophilus pro-biotic softgel capsules

plus a few other items I'm forgetting.

I'm still, even now, in the process of deciding how to tell my vengeful story. To make it entirely one-sided, all about what she did to me, me, me, victimized elegant alone-in-the-world bookish me, will feel good alright, but won't make for very satisfying reading. Anyway, the contours of her acts are all too deformed to explain to any normal interlocutor. Listening and comprehension itself are forms of sympathy. But it's a more delicate butterfly that I chase here. The chili'd chocolate of a Oaxacan village, sixteenth-century dust rising out of a palimpsest manuscript, fresh hot semen steaming on my leather chaise, these are the scents I want you to trace, like a fur-hatted trapper, my reader, on the snowy tracks of my unfortunate short life to date. An incense cone snuffed still, an orange blossom crushed underfoot, a paper snowflake run through an electric shredder-- this is what she did to my love. I did it back, double, to her life, until she twittered no more.

CAST OF CHARACTERS

XIMENA......a gentle lady
LUZ-DIVINA......her maidservant
PEDRO ALGODÓN......her protector
SEGISMUNDO......her faithful hound
TOWNSPEOPLE of various types

[The scene is at East Midtown of Manhattan, at a time of great unease.]

Not anyone's real names, of course, but not entirely false either. It would be more accurate to say that I have changed the names only so to render them transparent enough to show the personages beneath. From mask to powder blush: that is how you can characterize the names' transition. Like opening a set of Venetian blinds, with a flick of the wrist, a consonant or a vowel here or there moved a centimeter, reveals the Grand Canal in all its putrid magnificence. But enough talk of Venice.

The relevant part of the action starts on the even more putrid swells of Manhattan Island's East River, where, if you trail your gaze to the better shore and trace it up twenty-two stories and tease it a little to the left and squint to perceive the fragile figure perched on that terrace, you'll spy me, lost in a dreamy reverie, sipping from a small glass of liquid yogurt. Pristine as the day I was born (a day twenty-eight years ago, when I was pristine as an Alpine spring), neat, tidy, polite, emanating a glow of restrained joy. Today is the day I have finally moved into the apartment I've always wanted: a sun-dappled, hardwood-floored, silent one bedroom at The Cloister. The Cloister (not its real name, but this romp through the city of dreams should not require *too* much hand-holding to decode, and will, with minimum effort on the part of the cognoscente, run like a lady's nude stocking to reveal yet nuder truths) I'll begin again. The Cloister is a good building, with ingenuous Tudor detailing on the exterior, ultra-modern inside (like your narrator), with the fitness center, roof deck, and 24-hour security that every single girl requires, but few can afford in this stringent economic climate.

And even though you now know who you are,
and the delusion has been lifted from you,
and you find yourself in a place
where you are better than others,
pay close attention to my warning:
be humble and tractable,
because you may be dreaming,
even though you think you're awake.

from the Spanish Golden Age drama *Life is a Dream* by Pedro Calderón de la Barca, TRANSLATION MINE

Luz-divina detested the 4 train almost as much as she detested everyone who rides it between her stop in the Bronx and 86th Street in Manhattan. The sickly fluorescent light, the fat bottoms crammed into elasticized denim, the neglected hostile children, the battery vendors, the overheard cell phone conversations on the elevated tracks, the ads for immigration lawyers, the possibility of potato chip crumbs, were among her grievances on that trip. You could catalogue the things she hated about herself in the same breath: too short, too fat, not enough bosom to camouflage thick waist, undereducated, homesick, sentimental, born way too underprivileged. As a very wrong-place-wrong-time woman, her intelligence was almost a handicap, or had been until a certain moment. She hated being a Mexican cleaning lady, but not as much as she had formerly hated being trapped in the shittiest part of the periphery of Mexico City. For a woman in her late thirties, she was unusually optimistic. Luz-divina thought there might have been still enough time left to save enough money to go home, build a house, find a good husband, and reform her kids. There wasn't.

There were certain things about New York that were delightful: Riverside Park, Central Park, the coffee and muffin cart vendors, the excellent Christmas trees and high-budget Independence Day fireworks, the free Spanish DVD's at the public library, the gorgeous men, especially in Grand Central Station, and the Chrysler Building. She was to start her new assignment at the building where her Cousin Alvaro works, which is called The Cloister. He is not technically her cousin, the way North Americans use it, in a strictly biological sense, like they were mapping the human genome, but in the more cozy sense. Their fathers had played football together as children, and shared a chicken coop as adults. Their mothers had gone to church together. Cousins. Alvaro had told her that the lady whose apartment she was to clean looks like a movie star, but is actually a librarian. Luz-divina was deeply offended whenever any woman was described as anything better than attractive because she herself had never, not even on her fifteenth birthday, been seen by anyone as beautiful. That was fine with her, but she didn't need to hear extra about all the special joys that beauty brings.

Apparently, librarians earn very little money, not even much more than Luz-divina did, so Cousin Alvaro supposed that the lady lives off a family inheritance. That was all he knew. The walk from Grand Central to The Cloister is a remarkably pleasant one, Luz-divina discovered. The streets were quiet and clean, vibrating with orderliness. It was January, the sunlight was quivery and weak, but not absent. Her back was killing her, which was nothing special, but she wished it would stop especially that day, so she could enjoy the weather. That past New York winter had so far been depressing, freezing and constantly piled with filthy ice. Now the sun was back a tiny bit, and there was a path cleared for walking on the pavement, but the back pain was too much, like a rodent gnawing on her spine. She glanced at her watch, a pink plastic digital hand-me-down from that slut Evangelina, and took in at once the dual facts that she was early for work and had two more hours to go before being due for another dose of ibuprofen. Executive decision: more immediate ibuprofen to get through the day. With ten minutes to spare, Luz-divina overshot The Cloister, walking all the way to the river and the rows of bare, unblossoming cherry trees. They were strangely beautiful—even a suffering miserable lonely woman could say so. Plopping down on a bench, she looked up and admired the spindly branches as she dry-swallowed the rusty pills. She pictured them dissolving in her gut with the concentration of a prayer, then paused to watch the water flow between Manhattan and Queens, the light blue of the subway map made real.

…what in your shining years was gold,
carnation, lily, luminous crystal will turn not to silver
or limp violets, but…to earth, smoke, dust, gloom,
nothingness…
from Luis de Góngora's sonnet *Carpe Diem*

The Reading Room at the Hispanist Society was a boudoir to me. There I preened; there I relaxed. There I reigned as one can only where one is truly at home. There, for pocket change, milk money you could say, I was entrusted with one of humanity's noblest tasks: Collecting & Cataloging Manuscripts & Rare Materials [CCMRM, or C&CM&RM for the symbolphilic among us, to which I plead Guilty]. It gives you an idea of on just what a threadbare shoestring the Society's budget was dangling that the two vastly different responsibilities of acquisition and knowledge organization were charged to one humble servant. Well, I was only too happy to bear my load like the Andean slaves on the oxygen-poor Macchu Pichu highway, but— as dear ivory-toothed Pedro Algodón used to say— *Even butterflies need to eat.*

Eat I must.

I supplemented my modest living with a densely-packed schedule of for-profit dates that never ventured out of the privacy of my room and tended to require the kind services of a ball gag to quiet my piercing shrieks. There is a happy symbiosis in this kind of Old World romance, wherein I receive the pain I love and those who love to give it can afford to spare their wives who don't love to get it.

Whoever should have the pretension to say, *I don't understand how she could do that*, is disingenuous. To whomever should say, *That is a disgusting way to earn a few bucks,* I would say the following:

- Does anyone know what *disgusting* is until one has become old and decrepit, and one leans upon death's door? And do not the elderly in that situation achieve a moral clarity that precludes their making such insipid judgments? You don't know the meaning of the concept. You only grasp at it, like at your cheap diluted version of ecstasy.

- It was way more than a few bucks. It was class mobility. It let me maintain myself in the style to which we all, in our world, grow accustomed, whether we have such access or not. I have always admired Genghis Khan for saying, *I detest luxury,* but alas, I do not.

I adore the swing of the pendulum betwixt day and night. It is a metronome of existence, pacing us wisplike creatures for our inevitable passage from this sunlit world to that other, permanently black one. My name, Ximena, was popular with the medieval Spaniards because it meant, in the tongue of the endlessly fascinating Jews, *G-d has heard my petition.* And in fact, throughout everything, all the distressing awkwardness with Luz-divina González

Salinas, He never turned a deaf ear to me, and always gave me just what I deserved.

Busy as I was at the Society, I was never too busy to keep up my personal education. I read Calderón; I read Lope de Vega and other luminaries of the Golden Century. Whenever I came across a particularly cogent passage, I copied it into the small leather bound notebook that Pedro had given me for the anniversary of my employment. It was a wonder of bookmaking, a miracle of binding. Its pages had beveled edges gilded with what looked like raw molten drama—it sparkled in the sunlight like jewels dangling from the earlobes of an animated woman recounting an amusing story. My initial was embossed and gilded in the center of the front and back covers, a bullet's trajectory hitting the right spot every time. Here lies the truth as seen by me. X marks the spot.

I also used it as a diary of sorts, but real life being a trifle too uninteresting to document moment-by-moment, I tended to limit my entries to these literary scrapbook reflections and then just a few memorable personal reminiscences to pinprick and outline the constellations of my life, just the points where stars twinkled and shone, to jog my memory when I am old.

The pages were numbered, gilded, too.

Today, a snowstorm in the city.

As of yesterday, I have been in the service of Pedro Algodón for one glorious year. This chronicle begins with a record of my happiness in servitude, and gratitude in friendship. How I love him most dearly! Upon presenting me with this lavish token, el Señor put me through a series of exertions that were remarkable for their strenuousness and longevity. He also served me an incredible Andalusian sherry that was at once dry and reeking of rotting lilies.

Picture, if you will, a cute young Texas matron, enjoying a richly deserved, long-anticipated holiday from her infants—a second honeymoon, so to speak. She and her husband are gloriously and excitedly ensconced in the Dallas Statler-Hilton. Bill has called room service for cocktails, her ex-college roommate and spouse have joined them for an evening on the town, and, in short, she has the world by the proverbial tail. As she raises her glass to toast her friends and life in general, her eye catches the telephone, almost smothered by boxes with Neiman Marcus labels. With a sudden pang in the vicinity of the heart, she says, "Everything's fine at home, of course, but I'd better call the maid. She's just like a mama to those babies, but I'll just…" A frown puckers her pretty forehead while the operator performs her magic. The telephone rings.

From *Your Maid from Mexico, In English and Spanish*. Gladys Hawkins, Jean Soper, and Jane Henry. San Antonio: Naylor Co., 1959.

Cousin Alvaro, dressed in a swank brown uniform, was standing next to a glossy revolving door. He gave her the bright new gold key to my apartment, and said, "If you have any problems, come down here and tell me, ok?" On second thought, he'd come up with her right then, to make sure the dog was in its area. Riding up in the especially speedy elevator, Alvaro gave her a run-down of the basics:

- The dog is absolutely un-dangerous, a retired racing greyhound who was adopted already fully trained and socialized. It doesn't bark, growl, bite, or stink. Very sweet, named Segismundo, stays in a gated-in area while cleaning is happening, otherwise is allowed its run of the place.
- The librarian is exceptionally clean and neat. The last cleaner reported having almost nothing to clean; the up-keep is so exact between visits. However, she pays a lot of attention to detail, so you need to shift your focus to small things to work there.
- As we both know, her last cleaner was our Cousin Rosalba, who does everything extremely well, so this is the standard to which the librarian is accustomed. Had not Cousin Rosalba been

compelled to return home to take care of her ailing mother, you would not be here now.

Cruising up to the carpeted corridor, they got out of the elevator and into my apartment, where a docile silver-haired Segismundo was already resting in his little ghetto. All Alvaro had to do was close the railing, and he was on his way down to the street level to resume his endless cycle of signing for packages, calling apartments, and opening and closing doors. Stepping out of her shoes and jacket gingerly, Luz-divina took in her new workplace.

Everything was just so; nothing was casual. It was like a monastery: bare white walls, polished wood floor, no rugs, no art decorations, no refrigerator magnets, no wall calendars or take-out menus like at the other apartments she had cleaned. Spanking white vertical blinds blocked the sun. Pupils simultaneously contracting against all the white and dilating with the shade, she began to really see the details of this lady's home. The white-tiled kitchen was essentially empty; she figured I must eat every meal out. The living room was severely under-furnished, in her opinion, just a single clear plastic desk with a matching clear plastic chair, a white plastic laptop, and directly underneath a fancy crystal chandelier, a white leather chaise lounge. No printer; she figured I must print everything at work.

Segismundo snoozed in his corner looking like a blob of mercury. The bedroom, too, was white-walls-wooden-floor, with a neatly made bed dressed in pale blue, a woman's vanity table and chair made out of that same queer colorless plastic, and an old lady-ish tapestry hung on the wall. Last room: the white-tiled bathroom, clear plastic shower curtain— My god, she thought, is this librarian insane or what? How about just a tiny splash of color? Please, even a red bar of soap— all-white towels and terry robe hanging on the door hook. Though relieved by the pre-cleaned environment, Luz-divina was thoroughly antagonized by the absent lady. What kind of person would ruin such a beautiful apartment with such sterile and drab design?

Opening the door to the closet, which she expected to be the usual mayhem zone in these professional lady apartments, Luz-divina needed to blink several times rapidly to fully see what she was seeing. She found herself standing in a small room, with mirrors for walls, deep gray carpeting, and the densest assortment of clothes she'd ever seen. The depth and sheen of the black all around her was overwhelming. She stepped forward into the nearest rack and felt with her skin a detail she hadn't processed with her eyes: the fabric draped from those hangers was rubber, all rubber! Seeing her jaw hanging open in the mirror, she closed it. She also

sucked in her gut, as she thought she looked like a
real little pig from the side-view. Ok, the other rack
had normal clothes on it. And the shoe rack had
loads of high-heeled pumps where they should be.
Pulling open an eye-level drawer, she came face to
face with such beautiful, carefully folded lingerie,
like in one of Evangelina's mail-order catalogues,
that she felt overcome with shame. Her shock at so
much black rubber had evaporated, leaving just
complete inadequacy in the face of such perfect silk
underwear, and so much of it. All six drawers were
stocked this way with lacy panties, seamed stockings,
laced corsets. It was all too much. There was a lot of
black, but also other divine colors, like pale pink and
dark purple. Only a truly beautiful woman could
wear those. They would be absurd otherwise.
Unfolding a silvery silk bra, Luz-divina wanted to cry
because it was so tiny, weightless, expensive, like a
glass of champagne to pour over good breasts. There
marks the dividing line between women like her and
women like her bosses.

There was an establishment around the corner from my house, called Texas BBQ that had a neon sign with stylized blue flames around the BBQ part (the Texas was plain white). I wouldn't've set foot in there even to ask for a glass of water-no-ice on a hot day, even if you'd held a gun to my head, or tied me up in hemp ropes and beat me with a riding crop for that matter, but Luz-divina, that angel of Forbearance, that exclusive contract model for Scarcity, thought she'd hit the jackpot the day she'd stumbled on their $6.99 Take-Out Only Special. Actually, it came to seven-fifty-something with tax. The cornucopia in a stretched-to-capacity white plastic sac included:

- One half rotisserie chicken
- One half pint of cole slaw
- One large square of corn bread
- Choice of french fries or baked potato
- Choice of any can of soda you want
- Condiments: bbq sauce, ketchup, real butter, real sour cream
- Plastic cutlery and many napkins

That is probably the best deal in New York. Luz-divina marveled that this treasure be here in cotton candy land, but not her own neighborhood, where prepared foods are expensive and bad. She'd look forward to picking one up after sucking my dead skin cells and Segismundo's silver hairs off the floors of The Cloister. Any prodigal malcontent could eat it all at once, and throw away whatever's left, but that's not Luz. Thrifty from the day she was born—and the day she was born, she was so underweight, the midwife had pronounced her retarded—she gets a full three meals out of it. Yes, three square meals!

Meal 1. LUNCH. Half the chicken (a quarter of a chicken) and half the cole slaw (a quarter of a pint)
Meal 2. DINNER. The other half the chicken, the other half the cole slaw, the entire baked potato with two of three butter pats and the sour cream
Meal 3. NEXT MORNING'S BREAKFAST. The corn bread with the other butter packet and the can of coke.

She distributed the bbq sauce evenly between lunch and dinner.

A run along the river, a dinner of flounder and dandelion greens, an hour of reading in bed, and then the blank oblivion of sleep—those were the untroubled waters of my home life.

I had become cozily ensconced in my new home. It was nearer to the Society than my old home had been, and nearer to my image of myself. For once, my faded museum-quality tapestry did not look laughably out of place on its own wall. Never one to descend into complacency, I did maintain several other clients besides Pedro— to them I will probably not refer again in these pages. They were Mr. Borsellino, Mr. Kim, Mr. von Holdt, Mr. "Smith." [Does it get confusing when, in a situation of no one's real names, only one gets pseudonymous quotation marks? Let me explain. I have, throughout, altered and improved the names of my associates. It is only in the case of Mr. "Smith" that I never knew his true name myself, and even addressed him in person by a pseudonym.]

Seeing Pedro was a special evening treat. More often, it would be one of the four others. Mr. Borsellino, for example, was far from my ideal, but if I loved them all as much as I did Pedro, it wouldn't be work at all. It wouldn't be real humiliation either, to be technical. A purist in all senses, I was gratified by the gravitas of an odious constant like him. Which is not to say that I had any clients who weren't constant, because they all were. A dilettante could literally not have found me. No, only carefully screened and serious, very serious, referrals. It would have been extremely awkward for anyone to work with me only once or twice, as it takes many meetings to even approach a perfect handling. They wouldn't have been able to find anyone better than me, in any case. I figured that until one of the five of them (Pedro, Mr. Borsellino, Mr. Kim, Mr. von Holdt, Mr. "Smith") died or was transferred to another post, they would most probably keep me in active service. For this reason, I had no reason to see an end to either my reign as Submistress to the Select, or to my comfortable peace.

Yet one glimpse at the maid's home life is enough to make one never want to look again:

"That's disgusting. Must you do that here?"

Evangelina, a girl singularly gifted in pouting with her eyes, looks up through the tips of her chestnut-honey layered fringe at her little troll of a roommate. "Do what?"

Luz-divina doesn't know which is worse, backbreaking labor during the day or arguing with this twit by night. "Your bikini wax. Wouldn't it be better to do it in the bathroom?"

"Look, Lulu, I have explained this a thousand times. Once more: To do it right, you need to see what you're doing. The mirror in the bathroom is fixed to the wall in a certain position. It offers no flexibility. As well, the light is too dim in the bathroom. The light in here is brighter, and the mirror tilts. This is the reason I do my Brazilians in the living room. In a salon, it would cost something like thirty-five bucks."

Though not exactly a woman of letters herself, Luz-divina speaks a much more television version of their language, a little closer to what might be called standard Spanish. Evangelina's monologues sound gratingly vulgar. You can hardly even call it Spanish, more like Shantytown-ish. Luz-divina clarifies, "What you call 'the living room' is actually my bedroom. I pay more rent than you and Lupe.

You and Lupe share the actual 'bedroom'. This is the reason I have more space. I pay for it."

Untroubled by self-consciousness, Evangelina tears off the muslin strip on her inner thigh, only exhaling a little loudly at the pain instant, and holds it up to the halogen lamp to see how well she did. An impressive pelt. Smoothing cooling aloe vera gel onto the red strip of skin, she flips that bleached forward-falling strand out of her eyes again, and states gravely, "When Rosalba was here, she was very generous with her space. We were all like sisters. She was so kind and so gentle. She used to set out guacamole and cheese on the table that you now have blocked with your personal computer," – she says personal computer, not together as a phrase meaning PC, but with the stress on *personal*—"and stacks of papers, so I think you should think about the meaning of sharing."

Luz-divina stares at her blankly, trying to control what would be violent physical aggression were they men.

"Anyway, I'll be out of your way momentarily. I have to get to work." Evangelina is a waitress in a bar in the North part of Manhattan, that's all she has ever told Luz-divina. Probably Lupe knows more details, but she's never home, god bless her.

The day is chilly and
crystalline.
I transgressed and walked
Segismundo into The Cloister's
private park, ignoring deliberately
all No Dogs Allowed placards. That
was a wonderful treat: we sat
alongside the frozen, dormant
flowerbeds, contemplating the now-
distant Spring.

But just who is this Pedro Algodón who occupies that sole solid spot in my otherwise splintered heart? He is a studied and elegant sadist, a loving family man, and the Ambassador of a mid-sized country— known best for the mismanagement of its oil reserves— to the nearby United Nations. We have calm moments together, daintily balancing sybaritism with symbiosis. Moments like this one:

Sipping a small white sherry, the crisply pressed Pedro inquires after the private library. "They're treating you well at the new job?"

"Yeah, really well. They completely leave me alone. It's just me and these beautiful sixteenth-century manuscripts. I'm in heaven."

"I'm glad, mi tesoro." Neither one of us finds it incongruous that he should call me "mi tesoro", although it may at first sound that way to you or someone else. "I'm glad it's working out."

"Pedro, thank you again for all that."

"Nonsense. You got that position because you deserve it. Introductions can only help so much. González-Feinmann told me you impressed them all at the interview. Don't thank me again."

Ximena's dimples twitch as she says, "Ok, then…No thank you."

Pedro is now skipping through the spring rain in a yellow cab toward his own true pm; his soothing interstice is over.

Ximena opens her Accounts book, a spreadsheet document in the desktop folder called *Life Is A Dream* (which it is, especially when your own thoughts are thousands of times more vivid to you than the vibrating cells of the material world all around you.) Typing carefully, savoring the every impact of pink lacquered nail against white plastic key, she enters:

```
      wrists and ankles bound with
coarse rope/ gagged with embroidered
            handkerchief/
    flogged with crop/ derriere come
                upon
        US$1200 and no cents
```

According to the Immigration and Naturalization Service, nearly ten percent of all Mexican nationals are resident in the United States. This is the main reason why Alvaro is never lonely. Even when he's technically alone, he's not lonely. Even when the three sous chefs he lives with are out at their jobs, he can go around the corner to the Oaxaqueño place with great cheese, or the karaoke place with the waitress with great tits, or just take the 4 a couple of stops to where Lupe and Evangelina are living with Cousin Luz-divina. More than just an easy-going guy, he thought, as he pulled his shirt off over his head, he is one good-looking guy, too. That is lucky. You can't choose your looks anymore than you can choose your parents. All are chosen for you by destiny. He turned his back to the bathroom mirror to check on his physique, which seemed to be benefiting wildly from the new low-weight/ high-reps cycle, and to admire La Virgencita. Her colors were still bright. His cousin at home got the exact same tattoo of the same rendering of the Virgin of Guadalupe on his back, but he was too macho to use sunscreen outside and then she got all faded.

Alvaro's day was pretty boring, like most of his am's, but tonight promised to be another of his magic pm's. Ecuador was playing Argentina, and the karaoke bar had a huge flatscreen now. Yes. He intended to bet half a week's salary on this, but it's not about the money. It's about the beer and the fun. Tomorrow will come no matter what you do, if you enjoy tonight or not. He is one *chingón* carpe-diem *cabrón,* shit-colored uniform or no. His cell phone interrupted his thoughts. It was Luz-divina. What did she want now? He was tempted to let it go into voice mail, but then he'd be plagued with guilt all night. Bad enough she's ugly, worse yet, she's got kids and no man, worse still, she's on one of those crappy G-5 visas that have your balls in a vice, and it's not even hers, does she need to be treated disrespectfully by family? No. Cocking one eyebrow at the mirror, "Hello, cousin." [Needless to say, this conversation happened in Mexican, but I assume most readers to be fluent in English first and foremost.]

"How are you?" She sounded tense.

'I'm fine, Lulu. And you?"

"I'm well. Tired, actually, but I'm sorry to take up your time." Great, at least she realized. It would be short.

"No trouble at all, Luz-divina. What's on your mind?"

"Well, you know my main job, the Belgians?"

"Over at the UN, right?"

"Right, Alvaro. Today I found out from their babysitter, the Swedish girl, that they have been recording us."

Then he perked up because this sounded fishy. "Recording you how?"

"With a tiny video camera! Hidden. How disgusting! I don't like this."

Alvaro sighed loudly through his slender nostrils. These rich people always have to do something weird, even when it isn't called for. "Luzdivina, dear. Let's calm down first, ok? Is it so terrible that they do this?"

"It makes me feel violated. Raped. How can people scrutinize you when they're not even there? If she wants to know everything, she should quit her job and stay home." The female hysteria was flaring up again. Actually he agreed with her—it's a little creepy, but only a little. He didn't want to encourage anything extreme.

"Listen, Lulu. It's their home, right? It's their private property. They're the boss." Knowing that she can't quit, he couldn't say the gringo thing: *If you don't like it, then quit.* "Anyway, you do everything correctly, right, Lulu?"

"Yes, of course, but that's not the point."

"Just don't worry about it."

She couldn't help but feel like they're collecting evidence of some kind. "It just gives me grief."

"Sure it does, but it's not just them. There is surveillance everywhere here. Stores, traffic, elevators, ok? Don't get paranoid, my heart."

He had a point. The supermarket had cameras, too. Anyway, it had been misguided to call him to begin with. What could he do? "You're right, Alvaro. Thanks. Really, thanks."

"Don't mention it, Luz-divina. Call anytime. Take care, ok? Bye."

She wished she could find a good man like her cousin who would love her, but realistically, if he were not her cousin, he wouldn't love her at all. All men, every last one of them, like beautiful women. Malaise grew in her heart like a confused tumor. How much longer could she take being separated from her kids like this? Even the Swedish babysitter had the comfort of a lover on her nights off. Luz-divina never got any comforts at all.

Ok. Enough tedium.

Fast forward the surveillance tape, if you'll indulge the luxury of analog for a precious moment, to what could optimistically be called the best idea of Luz-divina's life, and what would realistically be called a novel, but ill-fated idea. Take your pick.

She'd been cleaning my apartment for a good while now, and never had any cause for complaint, as I had always paid her promptly, the agreed amount, and had made it clear that any time she had a personal emergency, she could re-schedule her hours to suit her. She would not even need to obtain my permission; she would only have to ring Alvaro and he would slip a note under my door indicating when she would next work. This was rather generous of me, as I never had that privilege in my work, and would have found myself out of a job, or two jobs, if I had behaved similarly at the Society, or with the gentlemen. However, I'm fair, and took into account that neither I nor anyone else was buying her health insurance or a retirement plan, so one makes allowances.

Now, bear with me, as I had to piece all this together in retrospect, from threadbare scraps of interviews, deductions, confession and conjecture. In other words: I could be slightly wrong, but not grossly so. I think we can all agree that my guesses about events that occurred outside my field of vision, told speedily, are superior to a long, slow, meandering patchwork process of how I chanced upon what, and to what degree it's been confirmed. Correct?

So, Luz-D, as I have taken to calling her in the hastily scrawled notes I use to keep track of events, was horrified, but morbidly compelled by the Flemish diplomats' use of tiny wireless cameras to record what transpired in their own home in their absence. This extension of the seeing eye, and the violation of the seen that it implied, seemed to encapsulate every trapping of power that had ever eluded her. That the technique should be so duplicitous, and that furthermore, it should lie so perfectly within their circle of entitlement—yes, that was at the crux of Ownership. That, all of that, was what Luz-D had never had the simple pleasure to experience. Plus, she was impressed by the pure efficiency of it. Minuscule and hidden, it had to reveal only an unrehearsed truth. It rendered the wall of time transparent; it converted the inaccessible truths of another's private time into a daytime soap; it opened the secrets of the heart.

She arrived early and left late from her next day at the Belgians, so as to allow herself ample time to hunt high and low for cameras. She wanted to know both from which angle she was being recorded, and what the recorder itself looked like. Was it shiny, like the i-pods of the whores on the 4-train? Or matte black, like the camera in a photographer's studio? Was it recessed into the wall, with only a pinhole for an eye? She never did find one, since it was too hard adjusting her gestures to make it look like she was straightening up while she searched. She wasn't a classically trained theater actress, for god sake.

That night, she arrived home burdened with a huge sac from the Mexican grocery, and set to preparing home made quesadillas and hot chocolate. She deserved a treat, after all this foolishness. She would make some extras for Lupe to reheat later, but not Evangelina. She could get her own. Manually grinding the spicy stuff for the salsa in a stone mortar and pestle, she had a thought something like, "I will not be deterred," though it was not clear from what she was being deterred, or by whom.

Mouth pleasantly on fire, and the apartment still blissfully empty, Luz-D sat down in front of her desktop computer with the second terra cotta mug of frothy cinnamonized chocolate that was to serve as dessert. She held it near her nose to let the perfumed vapor rising off it calm her down while she struggled against the grinding, dragging idiocy of her dial-up connection. She desperately wanted hi-speed access, but her building couldn't get it, run-down cesspool that it was. Consequently, she used the internet only on special occasions, for extremely important reasons, so as to save her phone bill and her sanity. The interminable waiting for every page load made everything seem not-worth-it and her life pathetic.

Searching for *wireless camera* was fruitful, indeed. She read and understood how it worked: **Create your own wireless video camera system!** With X10 surveillance cameras, we've made it extremely easy and affordable to look after your loved ones, home and possessions - or even just to have fun. Choose from our large selection of tiny wireless and wired cameras to keep watch over whatever you choose. You'll also find a variety of camera packages, all designed to set up easily - at prices for just about every budget. It even became obvious to her that there was an entire sub-species of camera called the "nanny camera". That Belgian bitch was not at all original—turns out they all do it, to make sure they get their money's worth, those lazy absentee skinny slaveholders. She breathed in the delightful aroma of the chocolate again. Must stay calm and relaxed on one's evening off. The FAQ's, which she had to look up on a Spanish search engine to find out means Frequently Asked Questions, were so long and dense that she fell asleep wading through them, though not before caving in to the urge to return hopelessly, a wretched somnambulist, to the fridge to gobble down Lupe's allotted quesadillas, smothered in the now over chilled salsa. What a pig.

A word on the Belgians.

He, Mr. van Hove, a nepotistic crony with a plum post at the United Nations, was supposedly an expert on Food Shortages, Chemical Warfare, Refugeeism, and Terrorism, or at least one of those, or a combination thereof. She, Mrs. van Hove, made a point of being exquisitely busy all the time, in an undefined way that underscored what a wonderful career she had been building back home, as a concert pianist or pastry chef or something that hands-on yet intellectual, before throwing it all away on the constantly adjusting and ever-displaced life of the diplomat's wife. They were both grossly overweight and fair-haired, the woman festooned with diamonds in outmoded settings dating from the colonial period in the Congo. Or so I gathered from eyewitness accounts, after we finally did meet and chat, by Luz-D, that arbiter of good taste and surrogate anorexic (only on behalf of others, who are too blind to see themselves as hideously fat. She was generous that way.) The children, apparently, whined non-stop, subsisted solely on Nutella, and played ultra-violent video games.

So, we are not to feel sympathy for them when little Lulu decides to order $1190.99 [on sale from $1329.99. Quite a bargain.] worth of digital surveillance equipment from the comfort of the ergonomically advanced German swivel chair at their home computer, using their credit card information, selecting the Pick-Up At Warehouse Super Saver Delivery option, then helping herself to two—two, mind you, not one—Linzer tortes from their fridge on her last day working there. The next morning, she rushed over, bleary-eyed with the kind of guilty anxiety that is so often a perfect stand-in for grief, to explain to them that much as she regretted to, she had to catch the next flight to Mexico City, then the next connecting bus to the Valley of Malinalco, to care for her aged mother who had just fallen ill. "I'm so sorry," she heaved. It would be one-way.

Well, I do feel sympathy for the van Hoves, as I feel sympathy for any victims of selfish crime.

Mark this, because lies are all too frequently shoddy containers for the truth, and the less well constructed they are, the more the truth leaks out.

My mother was tall and slim, with tastefully dyed blonde hair, blue eyes, and a smattering of freckles across her nose. That's all I know. I can barely recall her face at all, only that magazine-like description: "tall and slim, with tastefully dyed blonde hair, blue eyes, and a smattering of freckles across her nose". When I do try exceptionally hard to call up her face, I find that I'm only seeing that of her sister, my Aunt Suzie.

My father was also tall and slim, with black hair and brown eyes, and a black moustache. There are more photos of him remaining, so it's easy to see him in my mind. I haven't seen his many brothers since the funeral day, but none were as handsome as he, that was obvious.

Their story is suitably tragic as to grace these pages.

Herself an unhappy runaway from Idaho, my mother migrated across many states and held many jobs until marrying her major love, my father. The youngest son of a large German-descended family of cattle ranchers in Chile, my father was something of an iconoclast. Having disagreed with his own father and older brothers on a number of topics, he left them and South America, and got a regular job in a minor bank in Connecticut, of all places.

When I was a toddler of two years and some months, they left me with Aunt Suzie for a surprise conciliatory visit to the paternal clan. Aunt Suzie never told me the exact reason: Why then? What for? Why not bring me? Anyway, the flight from JFK to Santiago went without a hitch. I picture them holding hands, looking out at the city receding away from them, snacking on peanuts and tomato juice, or a whiskey. They're in their best casual clothes; it's the early 80's, so maybe a safari jacket on him and knit dress on her? Or luxe track suits on both of them? My mother has on her diamond earrings, the pinkish light of sunset catches in them through the window at the start of the flight, and at its end, the violet dawn dances between the South American sky and their facets. But like all human happiness, theirs was short-lived. After a breakfast of hot strong coffee and a warm empanada in the Transit lounge, their connecting flight—so measly, less than an hour, they could have rented a Jeep for the same price— crashed into one of the jagged blue-white peaks of the Andes that had been obscured by a thick hostile fog. So, that was how I became a double spontaneous orphan. The crash did leave some survivors, but not my family, and not the pilot. If the black box recording ever did reveal what went wrong with the radar, or the communications devices, or air traffic control, or anything else, they never did call Aunt Suzie or me to tell us about it. Their remains were semi-cremated at the time of their collection, so the funeral was, by necessity, low-key. I was given the diamond studs, and they remain the only evidence I have of my mother. Of my father, I have the black, glossy hair and the ability to act confidently on my own.

When I hear the word "family", I see a pile of rubble and ash smoldering defiantly in the frozen embrace of that mountain range so famous for its lost civilizations.

As a special Sunday treat, the ever-maudlin Luz-divina took her wallet-size school photos of her son and daughter to be laminated. She felt sorry that the Kinko's workers had to work on Sunday, the Lord's officially sanctioned day of rest. Even she never had to do that. Sundays, holiday or no, she spent daydreaming about reuniting with her two little angels from heaven. They were the sweetest children she had ever known, and she honestly didn't think she thought that only because they were hers. For one thing, they looked nothing like her. One couldn't even guess she was their mother. They looked just exactly like their fathers, two very handsome, if unreliable and selfish, men. For another thing, they had kind and calm temperaments, patient and pure. They seldom cried and never whined for things they knew they couldn't afford, like new clothes from the department store, fancy toys, or brand name sodas. They were humble, and like miniature saints, waited quietly for their beans, knelt in prayer at bedtime, and helped their grandmother with the household chores. At birth, they had each been given tiny gold crucifixes on thin golden chains, but for the girl's upcoming eighth birthday, Luz-d wanted to upgrade hers to one paved with glittering stones, diamonds or rubies. She would check to compare the prices. That would be extravagant, sure, what with all her other financial burdens, but little Mariluz deserved something, anything, to make her feel like a princess. Life is unimaginably hard for a little girl with a handicap in a backward village like theirs.

There wasn't a real pediatric orthopedist, or even a real orthopedist, or—now that she thought about it—even a real pediatrician in the northern sense of the word, available to them in Mariluz' toddler time, when her limp first became apparent. Then, after that, Luz-d had gone North herself and her frail, overworked mother simply hadn't had the time or the resources to take the little wobbler to the Federal District for a luxury consultation. The bus fare and hotel alone would have been too much, let alone the doctor's fees. Forget about the cost, then, of any recommended surgery or therapy. And who would have cared for little Luis while they were away? No, it was no use saddening an already awful Sabbath with these kinds of regrets. Her mother's policy was ultimately correct: to teach Mariluz to be self-sufficient, brainy, spiritual, and proud, to teach her to ignore the taunts of the other children, and the dark predilections of the elderly that she would never marry. Mariluz' grandmother was teaching her to be Good, and that would be a better life lesson than any perfected body could teach.

After the copy shop, Luz-divina thought momentarily about going to church, for lack of anywhere better to go, but decided against it when she thought of all the cute daughters who would be there in poufy pink dresses with satin ribbons carefully woven into their ponytails and braids, cute pudgy hands tightly gripping their mothers'. Instead, she headed home to read the dauntingly large, yet mercifully bilingual manual for the **Security Camera DVR Recorder** she had purchased in a moment of enraged insanity before quitting her "best" job. On the way, though, she had to stop at a great Italian pastry shop for a box of cannoli, tied with red wax string, to tote home to her lonely task.

Out in the windy evening, I was walking Segismundo along the river when I heard my name called behind me. Walking with a greyhound is so relaxing, I must have been in something of a trance, since by the time I became aware of it, the "Ximena! Ximena!" sounded a little frantic, conveying the sense of having been repeated several times to no avail. I turned around, scanning the walkers and joggers along the path. One jogger came forward, smiling. She wore a tight-fitting t-shirt that read OU REALITÉ EST LA. "It *is* you. Ximena!"

I couldn't believe my eyes. This adult creature, prowling the fitness path like any other Manhattan woman, was my dear old seventh- and eighth-grade roommate, Lindsay. "Lindsay! Oh, my god!" We hugged, jumping up and down together while Segismundo laconically wagged his tail. We had gone to The X School in X, Connecticut (You know by now that I don't like to drag beloved people and places into the mess that little devil wrought of my personal story, and anyway, names are not that important. Wherever Ximena is and was, X marks the spot.), a fabulous girls' boarding school on the X River. I still pay alumni dues to them, after all this time, like a mortgage on my innocence. By the time I was twelve, Aunt Suzie and that vulgar Johnny-come-lately "Uncle" Kyle, had had enough of me and were ready to send me anywhere they could. Lucky for me, their meager budget need not have dictated my future, as my impeccable elementary school performance secured me an almost-full scholarship to The X School. The shirkers needed only to cough up the cash for my field hockey cleats, rubber waders, and tennis racket, and to drive me up to campus each Fall, which they did with unrestrained enthusiasm. I excelled there, too. My valedictory address mused on the theme of "Hard Work Is Not Always Fun." You can say that again.

Lindsay and I had been not only roommates, but best friends—She had been salutatorian. We had been co-leaders of the Senior Hike along a particularly scenic stretch of the Appalachian Trail, where red leaves and blue herons completed an almost surreally captivating autumn landscape. Yet we'd fallen out of touch for the most common reason: She was truly wealthy and I had been only pretending. After graduation, she had gone on to a boarding high school in Massachusetts, and I had had my leash yanked violently in another direction.

Now, as we walked hand-in-hand along the urban river, we stroked Segismundo's snout and made plans to go home to our respective apartments, shower quickly (no hair washing), change into normal clothes, and meet in an hour's time at the mezzanine level of Grand Central Station for drinks and snacks. As I got myself ready, I was happy, but a little destabilized, as I really didn't have any personal friends in my new neighborhood. I had cordial relationships with all whom I encountered on my daily rounds, but it was rare for me to make a date with another woman purely for fun. Fun was a stranger to me, as it is for most lonely people.

I'll spare you the friendly dialogue. She had a Bellini, I a Kir Royale. We exchanged condensed life histories (mine minus a few dispiriting details) and the verbal CV's most Americans mistake for small talk (mine minus the bread-and-butter occupations). Lindsay was as chipper as ever, and as gladsome as one who's never had anything bad happen to her should be. She'd just taken a new job in Communications at the UN, and had just moved into a one-bedroom at The Skyline, which she absolutely loved. We basked together in the joys of the neighborhood, agreeing that it was convenient and dignified, if slightly geriatric. We promised to keep in touch and meet regularly for dinners and drinks. I forgot totally to enquire, as is *de rigueur*, as to whether she was "in a relationship", so caught up was I in hiding the fact that I was in five.

Of course, there were lots of better surveillance formats than the digital video recorder Luz-divina chose. It was clunky, unwieldy, and not so easy to hide. Technology had, by the chronological point of this debacle, already offered such innovations as receiving devices that forwarded live video to one's home computer, or even to one's mobile phone. She knew, believe me, she knew. One can say what one will against that plotting coveter, but not that she was stupid or ignorant. I figure she was cautious about having the images traced back to her address and her person. By planting a device in my apartment, and then reviewing the recorded data at the same locale, a day or two later, she allowed herself to see everything she wanted to see while maintaining perfect deniability. If it were ever discovered lurking there in its domestic camouflage, she could well ask, "How indeed did that get there? Have you tried dusting for prints?", knowing full well, all the while, that she had only handled it in her yellow rubber household workers' gloves. I'll go further and remove one pillar of suspense: I never did find anything out of the ordinary in my defiled sanctuary, but it was smart of her to think ahead to worst-case scenarios.

Taking stock in the commonly held assumption that the best home movies occur in the bedroom, her original placement of the monstrosity proved to be a disappointment, yielding overheard sound, but no image. She'd had to deduce over time that my bedroom was strictly for uninterrupted cherubic snoozing. Not knowing, as it were, what she was looking for, it took her quite a while to finally move it to the living room, where the way more rousing tableaux were taking place. That wasn't as easy it sounds, given the sparseness of the furnishings. She had to wait patiently—though what, one could reasonably ask, did she have more abundantly than time?—until Lindsay gave me a "housewarming present" of a bar station on wheels. Finished in chrome, with various sliding doors and compartments for storing liqueurs and bar keeping accessories, it actually went well with the décor. In return, I gave Lindsay a tremendous potted palm, which she all but picked out for herself by declaring her need for *something green*. Little did I know that a friend's generosity would serve as a breeding ground for a nemesis' aggression.

The odd thing, as if the whole situation weren't odd, was that Luz-d had not the slightest grounds for putting me under surveillance. Without a whisper of a suspicion of anything out of the ordinary, she started watching me for sport. She, my employee whom I'd never even met, except through notes and envelopes of cash, came to watch the intimate moments of my life with the detached, hopeful interest of a *telenovela* fan, hoping that what is seen in a favorite soap opera will shed light on the bleakness of real life. While I had still never seen her face or heard her voice, she grew more accustomed to my face and my voice than my own mother ever had the chance to be.

More snow has fallen.
The city's desolation seems to
echo myself. I had two sessions in
a row, or one ultra-long one, with
Mr. Borsellino, who seems to hardly
reap enjoyment out of anything at
all anymore. He left welts on my
derriere that will take a long while
to heal, I fear. At the druggist's
for antibiotic ointment, I bought
Segismundo a new toy, a squeaking
butterfly to bite. He'll enjoy
that.

CHART FOR REMOVAL OF STAINS

1. FRUIT OR BEVERAGE. Pour boiling water through the stain.
2. BLOOD STAIN. Treat with cold water before laundering.
3. CANDLE WAX. Scrape wax off with a dull knife. Place material between two layers of white blotting paper and press with a warm iron.
4. CHEWING GUM. Scrape with a dull knife. Use ice water to remove. If gum is hard, soften with egg white.
5. CHOCOLATE OR COCOA. Sponge with warm water.
6. COFFEE. Fresh stains are removable by laundering. Pour boiling water over old stains.
7. EGG STAIN. Treat with cold water.
8. INK. Try soaking in sweet milk first before laundering.
9. PAINT. Paint is best removed by turpentine.
10. SCORCH. Water and sunlight will remove faint scorch.
11. GREASE. Rub in lard well before washing.
12. RUST. Use bleach according to directions.
13. LIPSTICK. Use bleach according to directions.
14. RED CHILI. Wash well in soap and scalding water, and hang in the bright sun.

Picture the two of us, mistress and maid gliding by on parallel tracks, not racing, but each on her own line. Time flowed on, the ice-skating course of Winter giving way to the roller skating path of Spring. The Japanese folding-paper vista outside my terrace successfully made its switch from snowflakes to cherry blossoms.

Most daily life is drudgery. One need not be especially disadvantaged for that to be true. Was Luz-d's season any more crushing than mine or anyone else's? I can't say; I'm not a philosopher of the emotional brutality of the economic condition. I'll allow that it sucks not to have ready cash. It isn't necessary to painstakingly document the several months during which I went about my quotidian duties in what I perceived to be the privacy of my own home, and she lived in even more squalid circumstances than usual, owing to her having quit one source of income. It remains a mystery to me why she resisted using the Belgians' limitless-seeming line of credit to acquire some niceties she was lacking, such as electronic appliances of the non-surveillance bent, a new wardrobe, a set of luggage, that bejeweled crucifix for the asymmetrical Mariluz. I can only conjecture that she wanted to maintain the purity of her fuck-you message to the peeping Van Hove's, but then that flies in the face of the common assumption that scarcity and desperation leave no room for ideology. She was a special woman, in her way.

Some milestones of that period:

- An anonymous philanthropist donates to the Society an Inquisition-era map of the Iberian peninsula, thought to have been commissioned by someone who socialized with Columbus. It is fragile and valuable, and keeps me busy with its safeguarding, records, and display for longer than the layperson would guess.
- Luz-d receives a tatty letter by air post, which states that little Luis has fallen in with a bad crowd, and little Mariluz seems to need glasses.
- Just when you think it can't get any worse, a phone call proceeds the letter informing of Mariluz' case of possibly fatal hepatitis. The village "doctor" has yet to pinpoint which alphabetical strain of the disease has taken hold of the tiny liver.
- I do something I don't normally do, for the first and what turns out to be last time: I accompany Mr. Kim on a long weekend away to a frighteningly dull ski resort outfitted with the kind of knotty pine furniture, cedar tubs, and smoldering maple logs that are most attractive to those whose home countries offer a drastically different style of leisure. That set of days are a blur of rope burns, tears, and frost-decorated

forests, and ultimately tip me into the welcome precipice that is adding another zero onto one's net worth.

The first time Luz-divina viewed a session was a horrible turning point for her. In her life, she had been exposed to endless permutations of cruelty: abandonment, poverty, unrequited love, drunken beatings, freak accidents, disease, natural disasters, government and police corruption, overwork, discrimination, and much more, but never in all her life had she witnessed such calm, deliberated, and choreographed violence. She was nauseated. She was genuinely repulsed and offended. Most of all, though, she was confused. She had no idea where to file the visual information—mentally, that is. (She instinctively dated the resulting DVD's with adhesive labels and stored them in a shoebox near her desktop computer, without the slightest idea of what she would ever do with them, and no inclination to ever re-watch them. Call it thrift or the internal librarian inside every woman that made her archive them.) At first, she suspected that the carnival of the grotesque she was audiencing contained a moral element, like maybe this librarian lady had wronged this older man, and was choosing to submit to corporal punishment to avoid having her misdeed brought to the attention of the authorities, or their two families. However, when the next story unfurled in much the same fashion, but with a different older man, Luz-divina was able to divine it must be for something as frivolous as fun. That even after many more reluctant viewings did it never dawn on her that profit, not enjoyment, was driving my end of the performance vehicle, should be attributed not to her dimwittedness, or even naiveté, but more to her limited experience with whoring. In her mind, prostitution was inextricably linked to short skirts, heavy application of rouge, worn shoes, gum chewing, and ill-maintained tresses. Living in such close quarters with Evangelina had lulled her into a complacent assurance of her own ho-dar. So, not even after countless bum-swattings, chignon-pullings, stocking-rippings, cheek-slappings, name-callings, and floor-crawlings had been watched at 32x speed, volume off, did our little sex detective put two and two together to make an appalling, devil-pleasing four. (When, after the fact, I interrogated her, in order to patch this sequence together, she convincingly insisted that it never once occurred to her that she may have been tampering with my livelihood. She considered me too rich to ever resort to that.)

She mimed a crucifix over her heart.

Or she gasped in wonderment over how decadent is the North.

Or she grasped a rosary and prayed that dear Mariluz would never even know that such evil existed. Then the mental wheels we hear so much about, the ones that turn clockwise for good and counter-clockwise for evil, started turning.

A LADY MAID'S ADVANTAGES AND DISADVANTAGES.

Drawbacks to every situation in life—Hardship of service: temper—Temper a mutual cause of suffering—All are faulty—How the ill-effects of temper may be avoided—Who are above harm from vexation—Temper must be controlled—If constantly irritated change situation—Desirability of a peaceful life—We should try to bear all trials—Temptation—Causes of pride and want of feeling—Relatives, etc., a source of shame—Elevation to be borne with humility—Disputes with fellow servants—How to lessen danger from ill-temper of others—The best rule—Regular rest not sure—Being kept up late—Advantages of long evenings—Result of good use of evening hours—Late hours made to yield good—Hardships few, advantages great—Security from temptations—Freedom from care—Savings offer provision for the future—Other uses for surplus earnings—Intercourse with mistress—Leisure for reading, thought, and religious duties—At church—Pleasures of Sunday—Knowledge gained of life and the world—Balance in favor of advantages—Hindrances of very rich and very poor—Situation conducive to wisdom and happiness.

Luz-divina, my loyal maidservant, was feeling fatter and more defiled than usual as she cleaned my abode after that. Her humiliation, as abstract, unwarranted, and even theological as it was, deepened like a wine stain on a white skirt day by day. Vacuuming what little mercurial fur Segismundo shed would feel like emptying a mousetrap, while changing my white cotton sheets would repulse her with the certitude of emptying a bedpan. Though on the surface she was the same diet cola guzzling sad sack as ever before, on the inside she was undergoing a fascinating personal revolution. Something she saw flickering between the twenty-odd frames a second of the stationery camera work in that video series had corroded her natural dignity, and combined with her ill-treatment at the Belgians', made her feel, for the first time, terribly consciously dissatisfied with her station in life. It was as though her carefully constructed dream of feeling fortunate to make it to New York City, and fortunate to inherit Rosalba's cushy jobs, evaporated all at once, leaving only the unretouched truth of life's unfairness. I have felt some variation of that, too, at times. That's how I know. (When we did finally get to chat face-to-face, she was in no position to air such self-aware dirty laundry.)

But she never did anything passive-aggressive like leaving my long strands of black hair in the basin. My micro-cloister at the macro-Cloister continued to welcome me home with a stringent, antiseptic embrace after my peaceful days at the playground of appointment-only learning. I really do pity librarians at the helm of open-to-the-public institutions, where dilettantes wander off the street to deposit their germs on reference volumes and to gleefully kidnap circulating materials only to deny them the slightest right of return. The disaffected zaftig quasi-midget festered ill will in her gut the way I quietly bred helpful bacteria in mine. As I unwinded with a post-one-work, pre-the-other yogurt each evening, it never even occurred to me that I should be furrowing my brow in worry. Furrow, I should have done, as I do furrow even now, recalling past events. The prison recreation director, Mandy, informed me as recently as today at lunch, that I *look stressed* and *should work out more* for relaxation. In this grim environment, discussing medicine balls with her over boiled peas and tater tots is considered a pleasure.

My first in a long chain of unpleasant surprises came one sunny week in April when, in what first appeared to be the grotesquerie of Chance, *all* five prongs of my patronage star dimmed in cancellation at once. I hung out with Lindsay that week an unprecedented five times, developing something close to, I guess, a close friendship. We dined and walked together, went to the cinema, and I learned quite a lot about her. For instance:

She had recently relocated from Geneva, where she had been religiously dating a banker named Edouard, who would retire on the weekends to a family chalet outside Gstaad. Naturally, she would accompany him and came to know his large, by her standards, family quite well. There were two toothsome sisters, a father, a juvenile stepmother, a pair of greyhounds (good for them!), then a mother and wizened stepfather (on ridiculously good terms with their former spouses), uber-sportif twin half-brothers, and their hairless sphynx. Earnest, ashen, doe-eyed Lindsay became quite attached to the clan over time, skiing with them in Winter (though she felt the twins took unreasonable risks on the slopes), and picnicking together in the warmer weather. She had scarcely come to distinguish between the house's many staff members, let alone memorize faces with names, when one of the sisters, Chantal, the busty one with an all-year sunburnt face, had made a curious comment. The whole group had been getting ready for a health walk, and had milled about the salon chattering in their laced-up nylon boots, waiting for stragglers to convene. The father, turning to Lindsay, had enquired, "Where's Edouard?" As she smiled and shrugged pleasantly, and was about to say she didn't know, but perhaps he'd gotten side-lined by a work-related e-mail, or some such thing, Chantal had cut in dryly, "Check Costancia's room." The daughter had been given a brusque look by her father, but Lindsay had filed the intelligence away for future use. Who is Costancia? Where is her room? Why does she have a room here? Why haven't we been introduced? Thus armed with hunter-gatherer precise alertness, before the weekend had come to a close, guileless, fair-haired Lindsay had understood the epic passion between her lover and the house manageress, a non-descript female from Warsaw. They had been in love since before Lindsay had ever stepped on stage. Costancia, it turned out, had a surprisingly not-young daughter back home who was an excellent tennis player, and a husband in construction. Devastated, my friend had broken it off abruptly, opting out of the humiliating apologies that seemed to be in pre-production as she departed alone to the city.

Now, having transferred to New York, Lindsay had high hopes for a fresh, but enduring love affair, but none had so far come her way. Instead, she said she found a horde of married men of advanced pay grades making unwelcome advances as she tried to work. She asked me, rather unsubtly, if I knew anyone good, hastily retracting it with the logic that if I did, I would probably be with him myself. I just smiled in assent and squeezed her hand, feeling closer to her suddenly, joined by the perversity and hurt that was not my monopoly. Aah, Costancia, Costancia, do you even know the damage you did?

Dead silence. What is going on?
After this bizarre week of
cancellation, I had to take some
action. I mean, can these men be on
strike? There's something I'm not
getting. I sat down and called all
five in a row. And what do you
know? All went into voice mail.
None have called back to reschedule.

The deadening vise of misery was tightening gradually around the fat-padded protein-stuffed hole that was Luz-divina's head. Her personal rhythm of scrubbing, rinsing, starchy take-out, and futile stabs at recreation had come to be punctuated by soul-draining sessions of larcenous greed. What I mean: After much thought and careful deliberation, she had come upon a plan that entailed more cerebral work than she had perhaps ever done in her life. First, she had—using the dial-up connection that was so excruciatingly slow, she could get up and make herself mugs of café con leche during page loads—opened herself a free e-mail account with [not the real name] the login name of ximena@xmail.com. Bear in mind that this e-mail address was available only because mine is an unusual spelling and I use my work address (library@hispanist.org) for all official correspondence.   All unofficial business I conduct by telephone. Bear in mind that my clients are all super-annuated and technophobic to a certain degree, as well as paranoid about evidence of adultery and general wrongdoing. Next, the dear little malcontent opened an electronic bank account linked only to this new e-mail address. Now, she had *two* pieces of electronic ID, saying she was me. Never in her life had she come so tantalizingly close to being beautiful and rich. She must have felt like quite the cunning diva, quite the genius. She luxuriated under the cashmere blanket of her satisfaction for several days, paralyzed by her own good sense, before doing anything. Then she composed her first missile of a missive. I've never seen it, but events have let me reconstruct it pretty accurately. Why do I feel she used Courier font? I just do. I think she thought it was classy and learned-looking.

```
Dear _____,
I have been recording our nights.  I
have many discs.  If you don't want
me to send copies to your family and
office, you'll send US$20,000 to the
bank account below.  You can use 72
hours.  After that, I send.

Salutations,
Ximena
```

How they could have thought for a second that that pathetic syntax and grammar was penned by my hand, is beyond me. I have to remind myself that the elderly and the fearful possess a diminished logic. Twenty times five we know is a hundred. So that divinely lit gargoyle made an effortless hundred thousand dollars (or "US dollars" as she would have put it) in one clean go. Well, but how often have you heard of a criminal heart sated with a reasonable amount? Of a rapist content with one violation? Don't all killers secretly crave the designation *serial*?

She as yet had not even linked it to an external bank account. At first, the numbers on the screen, blinking a coded telegram of congratulation were enough. Later, she would want to fondle the dirty stacks of green.

Forced to quote again From *Your Maid from Mexico, In English and Spanish.* Gladys Hawkins, Jean Soper, and Jane Henry. San Antonio: Naylor Co., 1959.

Let us not forget that the lady of the house has some duties and obligations to the maid. If you tell her that she can leave at a certain time, please keep your promise. Don't expect her to change her plans and stay with the children on her regular night off just because you and your husband have had an unexpected invitation to dinner or to play cards. If you promise her a raise in salary, either give it when promised or explain why you do not or cannot do so. Have patience and be explicit.

If the lady of the house does not supply uniforms, wear your own simple, washable dresses or skirts and blouses. Be sure you have several changes of clothing so you can keep clean at all times. Your employer may give you an apron to protect your clothing, or you may bring your own if you wish.

When you live closely with the family, you will learn much about them. *Try to keep their secrets, and do not gossip about them to your friends or your friends' employers. Try to give them privacy with one*

another and with their friends, but be available when they call you. Do not ask the lady or man of the house personal questions that are indiscreet.
ITALICS MINE

Alvaro meanwhile knew little to nothing of his poor relation's turn of fortune, if you can call a profitable descent into moral decrepitude "fortune". As far as he knew, she was still enjoying the fruits of indentured servitude at the van Hoves'. Unbelievably enough, though, he ran into her at his local taquería, a beloved spot where the tortillas slide on the tongue like the inner thigh of a girl no more than nineteen years of age, where the *horchata* recalls mother's milk, and the *chicharrones* crackle like crack in a pipe. In other words: Way too rich for Luz-divina. What was she doing there? He felt kind of embarrassed, like a teen running into his mom at the mall cinema.

Resolving to mimic the face of a person experiencing a pleasant surprise, he greeted her smiling. "Cousin! Wow, hi. I never knew you came here, too."

"Hi, Alvaro. No, it's my first time. I heard from Lupe it's really good, so you know, I decided to spend a little more on myself for once."

Sound interested, sound interested, he reminded himself. "Cousin Lulu, did you get a raise or something?"

"Yeah...uh-huh. A small one." She looked down, a good simulacrum of shyness.

"It's all going well, then? The librarian's place?"

Luz-divina felt at that moment terribly exposed, the feeling of wearing a thin skirt without a slip in front of a bright light source. She wondered why he asked specifically about that job. Oh yeah, right, it was because he worked in the same building, and essentially worked for the librarian, too. No more sinister motive than that. She'd lie. "Uh-huh, it's great."

"And the dog doesn't bark or anything?" He knew it didn't, as he'd already been wowed by its ghostly silence. He'd never met such a silent dog before; it was almost feline.

"No, it doesn't make a peep. That's a good dog." At least she could say one true thing. That dog was probably the only discernible trace of good in the life of that depraved pervert. Of course, you can judge a woman by the quality of her kids, but by her pet? Not really, neither nature nor nurture was under her control. After all, the librarian seemed to have nothing at all to redeem her.

Alvaro looked at his watch conspicuously. "You know what, I've got to run. Enjoy your food. I recommend the *taquitos al pastor*. Ask for extra pineapple." He rushed out with a vague sense of foreboding about his kinswoman's fate, tinged and obscured by an undefined joy of being alive, connected to the feel of his shirt over his shoulders and the rhythm of his gait on the pavement.

For me, it wasn't just the money (although I'll get to the finances in a minute). After weeks without domination, I missed the Submistress lifestyle, too. Some in my position might deny missing the work itself, but I don't feel compelled to pose. Is it weak to seek company from unlikely quarters?

Who am I really? I'm a woman in petal pink lipstick who is utterly alone in the world.

Within my work relationships, I had lulled myself into a complacency bordering on marriage. Like marriages, they were entered into with a mutual enthusiasm and shared goodwill. Like marriages, they provided sanctuary against an indifferent world; they provided comfortable repetitiveness, soothing in its familiar tones. Delusional as it may sound to you now, Reader, I genuinely believed they *liked* me.

But, sure, the money was un-funny. For the first time, I dipped into my sacrosanct savings account to pay a credit card bill. I didn't want to have to do that, but, bafflingly, I had no idea when my clients would call again, and I couldn't face the indignity of a late fee.

I paced the floors.

I wrung my hands.

I skipped my manicure one week, then broke down and went back two days later when my cuticles became shameful.

That lean, nut-eyed conqueror Genghis Khan leapt to mind again. As much as he had cherished scarcity, sleeping on unpadded animals skins in unheated tents, he also considered the entire globe his personal treasury. Isn't that really the only way to embrace a spartan lifestyle—to dwell nowhere near the edge of the precipice? My own steed was galloping wildly toward the kind of financial vulnerability that makes me shudder. I tried to entertain thoughts of a second job, but quickly disabused myself of the notion. They all remunerated too little and required far too much exertion. Ironically, I didn't yet think of cutting corners by firing the maid. It remains a good question why that didn't even flit into my mind. Simply put, I suppose it's because I hate to clean, and I felt that the joy of living at The Cloister would be sullied by having to perform such chores. Or you could say that Providence, with her perverse sense of humor, enchanted me just long enough for her stage comedy to play out in all its cackling black farce.

Life always provides diversion, however. Even in ladies' prison, there are Special Programs and Pizza Nights. After all, how would we fully feel the night of our suffering if we enjoyed no sunlit strolls through peace?

The X School, that warm bosom that had nursed Lindsay and me and countless other spotless young women, had sent out flimsy invitations on bright green paper to its annual Egg Safari, a festivity closely resembling a hunt for Easter eggs, except that it was scheduled after Spring Break, so as to allow girls jaunts to resort hotels, vacation homes, and maybe parades and family lunches on the real Easter. There was also a strict non-mention of Easter in deference to the ethnic diversity and foreign oil wealth represented in the student body. Oh, and the dyed eggs were hidden along a woodland trail, instead of a great lawn. I vividly recall wearing rubber waders, a tartan wool skirt, my navy anorak and velvet headband, winning the Blue Ribbon two consecutive years. Like now, I was back then extremely good at everything I did, dedicating my every faculty to my current activity, and losing myself utterly in the challenge of the moment.

Each year, as I've said, I had diligently paid my Alumni Association dues, as a kind of respectability installment plan, but had never attended an event. For one thing, I had no car, and for another, no friends (well, none that could have attended, assimilated, and appreciated). All that changed when Lindsay called, suggesting we go together. I couldn't resist her enthusiasm, and found myself in charge of the car rental. I even bought myself a pair of hiking boots, that happiness prop for which I'd had pitifully no need in the last decade or so. I was delighted to find that the new models utilized a species of latex in the upper.

During the long drive up to campus, the frankness between us intensified with Lindsay's confession of having endured breast reduction surgery. She felt herself ideologically opposed to cosmetic surgery, except in cases of gruesome car wrecks, dogs ripping off your face and the like, but she had been having back pain, and had grown exasperated with the vulgar stares and comments of strange men. She hadn't told any of her current friends, and intended, I guess, for her admission to be something of a non-sexual love declaration to me. I appreciated it, more than she could possibly know. Then I did something even more unusual: I unburdened myself to her with a version of the truth close enough to reality to feel cathartic, but distant enough from it to avoid exposing the horror my life had become since the start of adulthood.

I confessed that I had been in a long-standing relationship with a married man, Pedro Algodón.

(There was no reason to murky the waters with the other four. They were all of a piece, and she would anyway get the point.) I told her that he had abruptly severed his ties to me, and since the affair had been of an almost exclusively passionate nature, I knew nothing about how to reach him—not even his home address and phone number. I didn't want to call him at the UN, I explained, because I still loved him, and didn't want to create an awkward work atmosphere for him. I didn't even know places he frequented in his leisure time, so little did I know of his life outside our time together. (I thought that was a pretty good approximation of the real deal.)

Lindsay commiserated with theatric grace. She grimaced; she pulled one cultured pearl braceleted hand off the wheel to pat mine; she cooed sympathetically. She then lapsed into another lengthy anecdote about a similar situation she had been in prior to the Swiss guy fiasco. Something about a married lawyer who commuted between Paris and Baltimore, Maryland, and who carried her soiled lace panties in his attaché case. I interrupted to cut to the crux of it:

"To make matters worse, he had been, you know, *helping* me."

Lindsay understood right away. Raising one slightly overgroomed eyebrow, she intoned, "You mean like a sugar daddy?"

"Yes, right. And…I miss that, too."

"Of course you do!" Sweet, kind-hearted Lindsay, who personally wanted for nothing, understood.

Feeling liberated and un-judged, I went on to unpack my dilemma like an overstuffed suitcase. Meanwhile, the road became more verdant and more scenic with every passing minute. I explained that he had cut off his allowance payments as abruptly and with as little explanation as he had his affection, and that I never would have moved into the swanky Cloister, had I anticipated this indignity (which I never would have in a million years). I explained that I simply needed to obtain closure on whatever rift he perceived had opened between us, partly for my emotional sanity, and partly to determine my course of action (for example, should I initiate the process of trying to break my lease and move into more affordable accommodations?). She liked that. *Closure* was her language. That prompted her to generously offer a favor that I have come to regard as a watershed moment in this hideous saga. Working as she did, coincidentally, in the same vast organization, she would try to unsuspiciously obtain his home address. Armed with that, she figured I could at least get the chance to waylay him one evening and talk with him. We agreed I should make my best effort not to seem too stalker-ish if and when I did so.

The Egg Safari played out as these things always do: its choreographed gaiety and unflappable cheerfulness deepened one's melancholy to nearly unbearable levels. Handfuls of good chocolate in nearby baskets lent momentary relief, and everyone drove away with a tear-streaked inner face.

That done, Lindsay and I returned to the rental car feeling accomplished in that we had hugged and cheek-kissed many of our former teachers, and had been told by many of them how glowingly beautiful we looked. Several of them, including the principal, Mrs. Hurlburt, had remarked on how happy they were to see that we had remained friends all these years. By necessity, we had replied that we were, too, and wouldn't you know, by repetition, it gradually seemed true. By the time we had come full circle to fastening our seat belts again, one could hardly believe we had been apart all these years, without a shred of contact.

Strangely hungry for real sustenance after all those sweets and all that adrenalized chatter, we stopped at the Old Chestnut Inn for a hearty dinner of shepherd's pie and a pint of lager each. If we were to drive all the way back, we'd had better not indulged in a second mug. Laughing and reminiscing, the cushioned lounge became so cozy that we enquired at the front desk whether we couldn't have a double room with two twin beds for the night. The clerk, in bushy grey sideburns, lightweight plaid shirt, and tortoiseshell glasses, asked us, "Sisters, are you?"

"No, best friends," Lindsay answered in a decided way. I noticed that if I had said it, it might have sounded funny. She clearly had way more experience than I in fun spontaneous trips with girlfriends.

"You ladies are lucky," the rustic gentleman assured us, "Wasn't five minutes ago that we had a cancellation. We've been sold out going back months. All the parents of the boarding school kids and whatnot…" He trailed off to let our good fortune sink in and render us beatific in gratitude.

"Yes, thanks," I said curtly, sliding my credit card across the counter.

"Ximena—" She started to protest, but I gravely shook my head to indicate that I would get it. "Ok, then, dinner's on me."

We returned to our winsome little dinner nook, and ordered a carafe of thick red organic wine. Drinking and flushing, we spoke of how unreliable men can be, even seemingly solid ones. It was agreed that they are constitutionally incapable of loving just one woman, and will seek out newer and more novel affections wherever and whenever they can, providing they sense little danger of being observed. Nibbling a little cocktail pickle, Lindsay slurred, "Ximena, you are gorgeous. A true knock-out." She looked at me with shining eyes. I kept silent, hoping this wouldn't morph into an anorexic envy-pity parfait, as so many compliments from women do. "Don't take this the wrong way, but I think I have an idea for you to do some part-time work. Just for the money. Just until you sort your rent thing out."

I inhaled slowly, in an attempt to sober myself and still my beating heart. I didn't know whether to be shocked, insulted, or relieved that my old school sister would suggest an escort agency. Sensing my hesitation, she added, "It would stay just between us. I would never tell a soul." I remained staring quietly, unwilling to say aloud that I had beaten her to the idea way back in library school. Besides, it would be far too complex to explain why, after years of paid submission, I would find ordinary escort work demeaning. I just would. She continued with the sloppy determination of the inebriated, "I have this friend, Stacy, who runs her own talent agency. She uses dozens of girls for spritzing perfume in department stores. I know it's so beneath you, but it pays relatively well, and you could do it on the weekend."

Oh. My lungs emptied like a punctured balloon. Thank god I hadn't said anything. She meant retail demonstration. Oh, jesus. Oh. I took a long gulp from my glass tumbler. My hand trembled from the near miss with identity meltdown. I closed my eyes to relax in a moment of pitch black. Opening them, I had another fortifying gulp, draining even the grainy sediment at the bottom. "Lindsay, that's a marvelous idea. Frankly, it isn't beneath me at all. What's good enough for an out-of-work actress is good enough for an in-work librarian!" We both laughed, smiles lingering to celebrate the exodus out of a weird conversation into a practical one. I asked her to make an e-mail introduction between Stacy and me, so we could get the ball rolling. I didn't know the sort of people who shopped in department stores anyway, so there would be so little chance of anyone recognizing me.

Then I remembered poor Segismundo, who hadn't been walked in way too long. His racing career had raised his threshold for suffering, but I felt awful whenever I tested its parameters. "My dog! Linz, do you mind if I make a phone call? I hate to do it at the table, but I forgot about Segismundo." She gestured vaguely for me to make myself at home. I dialed the front desk of The Cloister. A voice I didn't recognize answered. "Hi, may I please speak with Alvaro?"

"Alvaro? Sure, just a minute." Rustling sounds and shouts of his name.

"Hello? Alvaro speaking."

"Hi. This is Ximena. 22G?"

"Hi, Ximena. How are you?"

"Well, I'm so sorry to bother you, but I'm calling from Connecticut, and it looks like I'm going to have to spend the night. Could you possibly—"

"You want me to walk and feed the greyhound?"

"Yes! Could you, please?"

"No problem. I have a break coming up in half an hour. I'll do it then, ok?"

"Alvaro, thank you so much. You're a lifesaver." I hung up confident that my real best friend would be well taken care of. Alvaro struck me as a responsible man. I wondered for the first time if he lived alone or with a woman.

Scarfing down butter cookies with our tea like it was not a disgrace, Lindsay told me about her peculiar neighbors, a mild-mannered couple consisting of an American man and his Scottish wife, who would occasionally get extremely drunk and laugh wildly like hyenas. The next day, they would invariably take time out from popping aspirin and icing their heads to bake sugar cookies—from scratch—and leave them at her doorstep in a tin decorated with Dalmatian puppies on a tartan blanket, with a note to *Please return when empty. Enjoy!*

"Try Pleasure today. Pleasure." Far from one of the more humiliating things I'd ever done, perfume spraying had to be one of the more boring. Just to contextualize for you, this from a woman who took Advanced Cataloging because she got an A in Cataloging and was ready for more engrossing challenges. This from a person who has just recently finished re-binding and chronologically ordering fifteen years' worth of *National Geographics* for a group of sullen baby killers. Well, not all of them. Some of them killed their husbands or husbands' mistresses, I suppose. The point is, I have a remarkable tolerance for thankless tasks, but standing on my feet for hours at a time in uncomfortable shoes, blood pooling at my ankles, pursuing shoppers like a rapist, and olfactorily blinding them for a shrunken paycheck was not my cup of tea. Wearing the same arch-cramping footwear tied to a chair or bent over a stern knee, chastised into orgasm, for a comfortable sum, suits me far better. My compensation seemed hardly worth depositing in a bank; we're talking about the kind of numbers spent in one go on organic fruit.

Pleasure indeed. Confronted again with the obesity and hopelessness of the average normal American, I retreated into myself, using a familiar trick that had been with me since the bitter loss of my parents, and that had always served me well in times of physical crisis, when one feels better a little further from oneself. Water is such a numbing vision. I have this mental image of a particular swimming pool, frigid and over-chlorinated to the complete annihilation of all microbes, set in amongst snow-capped mountains, could be the Andes or the Alps, doesn't matter, just not the Himalayas. It can only be reached by cable car. It's empty except for me; not even a lifeguard sits watching. It is dead quiet, and only my shiny limbs cutting through the surface makes a sound, but the sound is warped by my latex cap, so my own movements are mysterious and exotic as the language of whales. Red stripes painted along the bottom guide me on a straight and perfect trajectory. I have swum there mentally for hours when I've had to, and I have had to for reasons you can imagine more vividly than I can tell them. I even sometimes mentally swim there while I physically swim in The Cloister's narrow, dark pool, swarming with groomed housewives like a fish farm pond with trout. Behind the reflective lenses of my goggles, my eyes reflect sometimes this vision of a place I've never been. From where did I get this fantasy? Who knows. From whence comes anyone's fantasies, those perfect dioramas of furrowless brows and bugless fruit orchards? I'd spent so much time deeply embedded in those five men's particular unforgiving fantasies that I'd cultivated a proud attachment to my own banal one, a travel guide book defined pleasure, a place scrubbed clean of noise and germs, where only fitness and sanity prevail. There I swam dreamily for a pair of weekends, until the next chapter came crashing down like a guillotine straight onto my flippers.

Linz (I had taken to calling her that consistently ever since we retreated into the Old Chestnut's hot tub together; and she had started calling me X) didn't elaborate as to her sleuthing methods, but sufficed to say, Pedro Algodón's abode became another of my known coordinates on this majestically cramped island. Naturally, I felt timid about accosting him there, so I slowly worked up to a gentle solution. I had to figure out his comings and goings schedule, so as to allow me to handpick a moment that would cause no friction with the family. Having a hardcore sadist at the helm of one's household would certainly be difficult enough, without having one's face rubbed in his infidelities. Pedro was also an extraordinary gourmand, and I imagined that placed considerable pressure on his wife and the cook, if they had one, to cobble together innovative and rich dishes every night. I resolved not to be a human problem.

His home turned out to be a stately townhouse, owned by his country's government, occupied rent-free as a protocol perk. It was, not surprisingly, just a five-minute walk from my place. I felt a new appreciation for our former arrangement—or was it not former, I dared to dream, was there just a misunderstanding in the works? A national crisis too classified to appear in the papers? It had all been so convenient for him. Looking at the stone façade of his castle made me miss him even more, and feel even more like his slave. If he were to lean out the third-floor window at that moment and spit down to the street, I would try to catch it in my mouth just to show him how I felt. However, I kept walking, conscious of being seen to loiter.

I analyzed the dimensions and sight lines of his block, like an assassin looking for sniper posts, but no—I felt more like a Secret Service agent guarding against the sniper. All I wanted was to clarify things between us. An act of Good. So, I reverse-engineered a surveillance post at the corner booth of a Dunkin' Donuts. Kitty-corner to his front entrance, the plate glass window afforded a perfect view, along with the non-negotiable nonchalance that comes with sitting on fuchsia and orange formica. I ordered an obscenely large styrofoam cup of flavored decaf, so that my length of stay wouldn't even seem out-of-the-ordinary to the cashier. Hours passed, and I observed his tall elegant wife leave twice— once in stretch clothes with a yoga mat, once in a knit suit with what looked like a real Birkin bag—and return once. A stout housekeeper type came carrying a large pink plastic bag from a discount store. I took notes in my gilded journal, feeling vaguely abusive in the process. The after-school rush was hairy. Hordes of nanny-guided pale children spilled in, whining for varieties of donuts that had been discontinued or were sold out. The way they ate the powdered ones left them looking like underage Japanese courtesans. A couple of precocious pre-pubescents in glitter nail polish and unctuous lip gloss ordered coffees with a certain gravitas, but then proceeded to stir in eight, ten sugars and return to the counter for "more heavy cream". That one exhausting afternoon has left me fearing for the future of this society. The cashier and I exchanged relieved smiles in the calm aftermath.

After I had caved in to a fat-free muffin, I spotted him. There was Pedro Algodón, magnificent in a light wool suit, no overcoat. He hadn't the look at all of a man most happy wielding a riding crop. He walked with a jaunty gait, the walk of a person in tennis whites. Did he pine for me at all? There was only one way to find out. Smiling again at the cashier, who, it turned out, was actually two copies of the same woman, two of three triplets from Dhaka who owned the franchise, I slid into my spotless white trench, smoothed down my hair where it led into a tight chignon, and dashed out to the sidewalk. I must have instinctively rubbed one of my diamond studs for good luck though I don't recollect it, so wildly did my heart beat. Not one to shout, I called his name at medium volume. No reaction, and he was getting dangerously near the front door, already groping for keys. Then I really shouted, feeling his name burst out of my lungs like an infected cough. "Pedro! Mr. Algodón!" He stopped in his tracks and looked around. I waved from where I was, not wanting to be seen from the windows of his rooms. It took him a second to recognize me, but when he did, the reaction could be discerned in an aerial photograph. Every cell of his body seemed to stiffen, a vestigial memory from his loins. Eyes darting momentarily to his home, he conspicuously glanced at his cell phone, pantomiming looking at the time or maybe receiving an urgent text message, and then made to cross the avenue. A man when he is escaping home is always a great actor.

He glided towards me and grabbed the crook of my arm in one fluid gesture. "Ximena, come this way," he hissed. We walked quickly in silence until we had reached the next avenue, walked south a couple of blocks, and ducked into another Dunkin' Donuts.

"Do you care for a coffee?" he asked somewhat absurdly.

"No, thank you," I answered him demurely, as if we had planned this using phones and monogrammed agendas.

"Herbal tea?" His politesse never quit. Happiness surged in my guts.

"Alright." I smiled wanly while he waited on line and paid. He knew enough not to buy any fried dough.

Facing each other at more of that tangy formica (this time as far as possible from a window, nestled next to the bathroom), he reached across the table and held my one hand in both of his. "Dear little Ximena," he sighed with terrible gravity, "how could you?"

"How could I…what?" I couldn't imagine what mis-deed he had perceived me to have committed.

"I'm glad you're here. I needed to see your sweet young face after that."

"Pedro!" Tears welled up in my eyes, and dripped soundlessly down my cheeks. I had never felt such solitude in all my life as in that moment, with the warmth of his manicured, wedding-ringed hands mocking my incomprehension.
"After…what?"

He looked a little puzzled, but only said cryptically, "I paid the money not because I was afraid. Not at all. I only paid because I wanted you to have it if you needed it."

"What?" I sobbed, "What money?" gripping his hand as tight as I could.

I can't report verbatim what was said after that because it all became a nauseous blur, a torrent of words and facts more surreal than enlightening. I'm only lucky I didn't faint. He narrated having received a blackmail e-mail (sorry for the vicious rhyme, but I think he might've said it that way) from

Me, demanding a medium-sized sum of money in exchange for My silence. I, apparently, had made him aware that I had been recording our sessions, and would make them available to his wife, exposing him at once as a brutal sadist, an adulterer, a habitual liar, and a whoremonger, in the event of non-payment. I'd never been so dazzled by fiction in my life. I stammered, biting my tongue in the process, trying to formulate the right questions to figure out what was going on. Mine was a confusion you just can't fake.

He freed one of his hands to drain the container of what must have been extremely hot coffee (I had heard him order it black; the lid had been on the whole time; the container said **Caution! The beverage you're about to enjoy is extremely hot!**) and to pointedly stare at me. I liked the effort he was making to re-order reality. Someone else would've just stood up and stormed out in exasperation. He was the sort to slap me across the face very deliberately, but never out of anger. I remember him finally saying something like, "Do you mean to tell me you have no idea what I'm talking about?" and me replying hysterically, "None! No idea!"

He then walked me through the rubble, gingerly. I was numb, adrift, and erased. My feeling was the feeling you can never understand unless you've had your entire family killed in a massacre, or you traveled in space, or you woke up in a hospital room after a 30-year coma, or you meditated until you understood exactly what they mean about grammar shaping experience. In short, I was in shock. Poor, patient Pedro couldn't tell me the source of all this. He could only pull a gold-plated, beautiful pen out of his inside breast pocket and write down on a napkin the e-mail address from which he had received the threat and to which he had electronically transferred money. With that, he kissed me forlornly on the forehead and strode away towards the townhouse with the family in it, and undoubtedly, a hot dinner.

I sat down at my lucite desk to think hard in slippers and a ponytail. At last, one plus one plus one plus one plus one began to equal five. Surely whatever had transpired with Pedro had happened to all five of them. Someone with intimate knowledge of our dealings had posed as me and perpetrated blackmail against all five of them. That much was clear. However, the crystalline waters of truth were still running murky where the Who was concerned. I got the bottle of cheap white sherry I had bought myself out of the freezer, and poured myself a brimming glass. How could I fear a hangover when my whole life was unraveling like an over-dry-cleaned knit dress? My laptop glowed ominously in the silence of my room. I tried to log onto My e-mail, which was supposedly linked to My bank account, but of course they prompted for passwords. I tried the first few ones to pop into my mind, gamely playing along with the idea they were Mine:

- segismundo
- calderon
- cloister1
- ximena

That was fruitless, so I tried to walk into the stroll park of the problem through another entrance, the threat. Whoever this criminal was, she (well, it could have been a he, but I doubted it. I smelled perfume all over the technique) was claiming to have video clips of my sessions. My mind walked on slowly and circuitously, hands clasped behind its back. She could be bluffing, and be only in possession of the *fact* that I hold sessions with these men. In that scenario, she would only need to have observed us somehow, but how? My twenty-second floor window onto the river could hardly facilitate voyeurism. Anyway, assuming, just assuming, she had some kind of peephole-like visual access, how would she have contacted them? How would she know who they were and how to reach them? No, too difficult, that would require near professional-level research skills. I knew about research skills. What, would she have taken their snapshot and run it through some photo database? Give me a break. No. She would need also access to my own laptop and my real e-mail account, where their names and e-mail addresses were waiting to be plucked like ripe plums. Assuming then that this she had access to my computer, my mind looped back to the tree-lined gravel path of the video. Without the video she claimed to have, what good were her threats? What if one of my clients, all intelligent and discerning men in their own rights, demanded proof? Wouldn't they, after all? And wouldn't her whole scheme evaporate like so much morning mist under the hot sun of their scrutiny? Though it sent a horrible chill down my spine, I knew I would have to assume that the video did exist. My mind turned away from the Who path for the time being. First priority was How. Walking now through the arid, desperate rectangle of a rock garden, my mind could only come up with *hidden camera* as a concept. I assure you that *hidden camera* was as alien a concept to my world as *monkey wrench* or *in-vitro fertilization* would have been. How did I ever even think of a hidden camera? What would it look like? I would find out. I started systematically tearing my home apart, trying to be as painstaking as I'd read Cold War diplomats had been in their bug hunts. I started by pulling my precious tapestry from the wall, in search of a missing chunk of wall. No. Then I proceeded to dismantle the chandelier, unpack my beautifully arranged closet, rip off the bed linens, unmake the dog bed, and even open and close the blinds in a display of manic futility. Finally spent, I decided to switch to cognac. My wrist was an inch from the chrome bar when it hit me like an injection of someone else's prescription drugs. Uh. I set my glass down gingerly and rifled through the numerous crevices of the cart until a foreign object winked at me with lascivious glee. A true and careful masochist, I decided not to dismantle it straight away. Aha. Aha!

I poured that cognac after all. Collapsing into my lucite throne, I drank deep and pondered even deeper.

I thought I might have a brain aneurysm staring into the tiny glistening lens, and imagining only bad things. Again, my mind provided a concept I thought belonged only to others: *inside job*. It had to be an inside job, someone who had a copy of the keys. Only Alvaro and the maid, although it was possible they had been stolen from one of them. Possible, but unlikely. How would a key thief know where to go and what to do without their complicity? He wouldn't, so again it boiled down to them. I shuddered.

Then, I decided to think about it in the morning. Being a double spontaneous orphan, I'm really good at falling asleep when it seems I shouldn't be able to.

Let's keep updated on Luz-divina through all of this, shall we? We can't forget our bloated, squat star.

Like a textbook case poor person, she didn't quite know what she would do with her modest fortune. She had yet to figure out exactly how she would convert the digital to the real, as she had no one to consult on the matter. Perhaps she figured she would link the online account to a Mexican bank some time in the future. In the meanwhile, she instead concentrated on repeating the performance and making the number bigger. Surely these rich men had lots more ready cash to spend and lots more to lose if exposed. She understood that she had asked for too little when not a one of them bothered to challenge her to show him the evidence. They had all just paid up the way they probably paid their monthly credit card bills without scrutinizing individual charges. Its ease mocked her as much as life's difficulty usually did.

So, as the bank statements clearly stated—when I finally got access to them—she went through the blackmail-appeasement charade three more times before I caught up to her. Interestingly, she asked for incrementally decreasing sums, quite the opposite of what one would expect from a greedy peasant. She figured, I'm figuring, that asking for more might risk stepping over an invisible trip wire, setting off a silent alarm of indignation, while smaller figures would just feel like additional annoyances to the men, unavoidable aftershocks. Her logic was exquisite in a retarded way. In this way, she collected ten thousand, then five thousand, then 2500 dollar packets of bliss from all five.

She was too accustomed to wretchedness to even splurge on a great haircut or new shoes. Some people that out of the loop often don't even know where to get a great haircut, or what kind of shoes fit them best. Luz-divina was one of those. She was no doubt saving the money in her mind for some miracle treatment for her little girl, an admirable goal, if it had ever come true. She did buy a calling card, and at six cents per minute, cooed into her mother's and children's ears that she intended to come home soon, maybe for good! She made little kissie noises into the phone, and told them how hard she was working only for them, and for no one else. She was, I think, a good mother, in that she thought of those children constantly, always scheming to prevent them from turning out like her.

The next morning, I called in sick to the Society for only the second time in my career. (The first time had been the Algodón stake-out day.) I felt awfully guilty about it, but I would be too distracted by the exigencies of this mess to be of any service there. I knew instinctively that Alvaro would not have betrayed me—my understanding of men processes on a DNA protein level; women problems get re-directed to my mind—but I had to be perfectly sure before I could proceed to the real work. I rang downstairs and asked if Alvaro could come up and help me with something. Not an unusual request, as underfed, overprivileged tenants of both genders often asked the concierge staff to help them lift, move, and open things. I waited at my desk impatiently, in a light spring dress and open shoes. When he rang the doorbell after what felt like hours, I re-arranged my worry mask into a happy, unperturbed one. "Come in, Alvaro. Hi!"

Having re-arranged the rolling bar to re-camouflage its arsenal, I discreetly grilled him on how things were going with him, personally. Did he like his job? Was he adequately paid? Did he often receive tips? Yes, yes, and yes, he truthfully replied. It took me a minute to realize that he was interpreting this de-briefing as a seduction. Ha! My first impulse was just Ha!, but my second, slowly dawning reaction was that one needs allies during trying times of life, and the closer one's allies are to the problem, the more useful they are. I looked him over carefully. If the Cloister had become a battleground, wouldn't it be useful to have a nice, young, fit foot soldier right within it?

Intercourse with Alvaro was relaxing, if boring, like getting body work at a hotel spa where the masseur doesn't want to hurt you. I'd always thought him a handsome man, but had never bothered to imagine his body, which turned out to be splendid, even breathtaking. I didn't mind the tremendous tattoo, edging as it did toward the fetish border, but if I were him I might have gone for something pre-Colombian, rather than a symbol of colonial oppression, but hey. He was a beautiful man, not dissimilar from my father photographs.

Afterwards, as he rushed into his uniform, I "casually" (casual has wider limits in the perception of post-coital, unattached men) asked him a few questions about my housecleaner, his cousin. Did she have many other jobs? Did she earn enough to get by? Any family? And, oh yes, one more thing, would you write down her local address for me? I owe her some money, and promised to send a money order. I had him write it directly into my gilded notebook, so I wouldn't misplace it. I glanced at it to make sure it was legible (it was, he had a fine hand) and kissed him goodbye.

I let my sense of humor toy with my good sense as I decided whether to erase the Alvaro footage. That afternoon was Luz-divina's time slot, so of course I would look around her interior while she was in mine. That was the only way to be sure she wouldn't be home when I came calling. Assuming, astutely as it turns out, that she would be collecting data from that hideous hardware, I had to consider whether I wanted her to know that I had recruited her cousin so absolutely. The sadist in me would've liked to cause her torment with the graphic movie (after downloading the manual and reading about its superb audio, I had turned up my own shrieks and moans), but my inner pragmatist said she already knew too much. It would be in my best interest to start investing in her ignorance. So, I dutifully reversed over the recording, marveling at how photogenic my legs are, and replaced it with a scene in which I pour myself a cognac and unknowingly block the camera lens with the bottle.

I got on the uptown 4-train, and stayed on for an inordinately long period. It would have been excruciating without the beautifully-bound Lope de Vega to flip through.

El castigo sin venganza.

Este ha de ser un castigo/ vuestro no más, porque valga/ para que perdone el cielo/ el rigor por la templanza

Punishment without Vengeance

This is to be only your punishment, so that it may serve to make heaven pardon its harshness with temperance.
TRANSLATION MINE

One word to describe Luz-d's abode: ewwww.

That worked in my favor because though I had no good excuse to be there, I knew that my off-the-charts out-of-placeness gave me a certain green light to enter. I've lived in enough bad buildings to know how authoritative great clothes and grooming look while standing inside them. No one would throw me out of there.

I rang the doorbell of the superintendent, who seemed to be on his last legs, in every sense of the phrase. I gave him an unrehearsed, feeble story in literary Spanish about needing to enter 4F. I was a distant (very distant) cousin of "the girls"—Alvaro had told me she had two roommates, so I figured I would hedge my bets by loosely linking myself with all three. He didn't bother to feign curiosity or interest; he could only cobble together enough energy to stare pointedly at my rump as I walked ahead of him up the four flights. He turned at the door and left without another word, obviously unconcerned about if and when I left, and how I would lock up on my way out, assuming I hadn't just moved in forever.

I won't numb your sensibilities with close descriptions of the interior. There was fluorescent overhead lighting, plastic storage crates used as furniture, and the kind of glue pads for trapping vermin that I had often used as a metaphor for my life, but never actually seen in use. The out-of-date desktop computer immediately grabbed my attention mostly because it was the only object in the apartment that didn't scream stupidity. It lit up when I touched a key. Encouraged, I sat down at the desk and tried to open her web browser to peruse the history, but I was appalled to discover that she actually used a dial-up connection. It was like a detail a production designer would think of to make a film seem convincingly in the past. What's the point? I think I would rather use a shared terminal in the public library…unless she didn't even have a library card. I would have to get used to shuddering at unpleasant thoughts, as I seemed to be doing it more and more often. I looked around frantically for a phone line, but my tension at being caught there, along with the general clutter, made it hard for me to pick out. Oh, there. It was a ridiculous looking plastic touch-tone in the shape of a cat. I plugged in and began the interminable process of connecting. As it gasped through the motions of telecommunication, I looked around more carefully, opening drawers and rifling through stacks of crumpled paper. I was hoping she had jotted down the passwords to the criminal accounts, but she was too clever for that. There were receipts for cash wire transfers of trifling sums, expired flyers for various church events, nothing useful. Then, my eyes finally registered a primly closed shoebox from one of those made-in-China chains. It was remarkable only because it wasn't in disarray like everything else, and was in a curious position at what would be the elbow of the mouse clicker.

There was her personal library of my torment, the archive of my humiliation. The fine hairs on my forearms stood up instantly to tell me what I was seeing. I picked one at random, and put it in her drive. It started right away, no credit sequence, needless to say. Yes, there I was, appearing to perform something that had never been performed; it had been authentically felt. Really, you don't know disconcerting until you've watched yourself at your maximum private, heard yourself at your most spontaneous. It was transfixing. Clocking the time, I checked the progress of the connection again, and was chagrined to find it had crashed, and was "trying again". Please try harder, Principal Hurlburt used to say whenever a girl said she was trying. I rummaged around in the desk drawers for a shopping bag large enough to hold the shoebox. My leather clutch was way too small to hold all the DVD's even if I ditched the receptacle and the jewel cases. Nothing. I went to the kitchen, figuring that these types surely horded good plastic bags for bringing out the garbage. I had to snort at the inspirational magnets on the fridge. Uh-huh, Jesus loves you with a pure heart. Just as I came upon their cache, the front door flew open, and a shrill little voice demanded to know why it was unlocked. I stepped back into the main room, where a slutty little beauty with citrusy streaked hair stood, hands on hips. "Good day," I smiled my my-Spanish-may-be-nerdy-but-you-understand-it smile.

She looked at me horrified, and I instantly knew I would have to modify the cousin story. "What are you doing here?" she demanded, throwing her gold leather bag onto the floor rather aggressively. She had gold lacquered long nails, too.

"Hi. I'm Luz-divina's computer teacher…" I paused there to let her fill in some credible details, but she didn't cooperate.

"Computer teacher?" He swollen lips looked like they would burst with contempt as she said this.

"From the New York Public Library." Her face started to soften only because I at least hadn't named

something preposterous, like a prestigious academy.
I continued with confidence, "She asked me to come
over and collect some of her homework disks. For
the Final." I smiled again, with the dry, saccharine
expression I've seen on the faces of many public
librarians.

"Oh. I'm Evangelina. Nice to meet you."

I shook her hand formally. "Likewise. Florencia.
Um, I'll get going. Do you have a large plastic bag I
could use to carry this?" I gestured to the shoebox,
which was fairly pulsating with menace. As she flew
into the kitchen, I flipped off the computer's power.
Abort mission. The tiny temptress returned with a
shopping bag from the same store as the absent
shoes. It was kind of touching, like a wretched set of
matched luggage.

When Lulu returned home from my home, thereby completing destiny's symmetrical figure-eights, she bore her latest installment of the Ximena Peepshow, another yawningly actionless episode. As alarmed as she was to find her shoebox gone, that was nothing compared to the alarm she would feel late that night, around three a.m., when Evanglina finally tripped across the threshold, reeking of cigarettes and rum. Her drunken announcement that "Florencia" had come by to pick up the homework, made no sense except the sickening geometry of Wrong. Lu-di grabbed the little *ruletera* [I had to look it up, too. It meant "itinerant prostitute".] by the shoulders, demanding, "Who's Florencia?"

She wasn't too drunk to register condescension and contempt. Sucking in her cheeks slightly, she stated as if stating the obvious, "Flor-en-cia. The teacher?"

Lulu shook her shoulders hard, like abusers do to crying babies. "What teacher?"

"From the library?" Her question mark meant *Idiota*.

"What?" Luz-d let go of her shoulders abruptly, and Evangelina stumbled to her knees.

"I'm tired," she mumbled.

Our Lulu sat down at her desk with a box of coconut cookies to think. The library clue tipped her off to the fact that Florencia had something to do with me. She didn't necessarily make the connection that Florencia *was* me, but that she was probably my emissary. Belatedly, finally, for the first time, she began to worry. As well she should have. You don't cross a double spontaneous orphan and expect to escape damage.

That night, she wore herself out with worry. By dawn, she was covered with crumbs and bleeding from the cuticles. She felt the enormity of being Bad weighing down upon her, grinding her flesh down, further and further from heaven. When it came to feel like a reasonable hour to start calling people, she dug out the number of Alejandrina, the clairvoyant seer who had accurately predicted Rosalba's mother's cancer. Lulu had never been to her before, but had heard that she was a magically gifted genius. She didn't come cheap, but everyone said she could tell you what was really going to happen. Specifically. She was sure to be a snob, too, like everyone from Caracas, but there was no else to whom to turn.

She was able to get an emergency appointment, one hour before Alejandrina's first appointment of the day. She stood under the shower without mustering the energy for soap, then threw on a t-shirt and a pair of the most horrible looking blue sweatpants. She walked stiffly to the oracle's live/work space, which sat above a video store. Alejandrina smiled kindly as she opened the door to her, no doubt conscious that emergency appointments are never for anything good. She decided not to really look into or think about this new client until she had served her a strong coffee. This person looked terrible, like she needed it.

Luz-d sank into a green velvet couch while Alejandrina puttered in the kitchen. She looked around at the normal furnishings and doilies and the normal trappings of the occult: a Jesus clock, unlit candles, jars of herbs. Everything was banal except Alejandrina herself, who was impressive. The seer was uncharacteristically slim. Lulu liked that. She felt that most seers' obesity undermined their ability to hand out life-altering dictates. After all, if you're so sagacious, wouldn't you have figured out how to slim down by now, thereby raising your average salary, widening your pool of marriage partners, minimizing health risks, and looking better? This one was even exceptionally thin, like she got that way not through the dual virtues of diet and exercise, but because seeing boosted her metabolism to a raging calorie inferno. She emerged with the tray of cups and saucers, cream and sugar, and the coffee pot, all done in a cute rose pattern. No cookies.

Now she held Luz-divina's hand and stared fixedly into her face. "You're in trouble."

Duh. Lulu stayed silent, waiting for more. She didn't want to volunteer any information, but she'd answer truthfully any question posed to her.

The oracle kept looking, with an expression of dismay starting to distort her small, bird-featured face. "You have an adversary. She's stronger than you."

"Yes!" Lulu couldn't help affirming the facts. She was right on target.

Alejandrina pinched her face in even more, squinting. "If she perceives that you're weak, she'll harm you, but if you show her your strength, she won't."

"But what does that mean?"

The woman paused to clarify her thoughts. "You have to act first, before she does. Aggressively."

"Aggressively?" Luz-d drained her cup in one long gulp.

"Sometimes brutality is not evil. You must do something brutal to show her you're not a victim."

"What kind of brutality?" she enquired, wide-eyed.

"Just destroy what she loves most. Then she'll leave you in peace." Alejandrina's cell phone erupted with a loud custom ring-tone that Lulu couldn't quite place. Was that a marimba? She averted her eyes and prepared herself another coffee to let the seer know she could take her call without causing offense.

"Yes," Alejandrina spoke into the glowing phone, "Yes. Yes. Yes. No problem. Ok, then. Yes. I'll pray for you." Then, turning her attention back to the wretch before her, "Sorry about that. And another thing. This is important."

"Yes?" Lulu broke off lapping at her creamy drink so abruptly that she wore a faint coffee milk moustache.

"You must leave here. Go home. Your family needs you."

She knew it. Luz-d always knew that there was no good place for her in the North. She needed to be with her children, her little hearts. She stared down at the hands writhing in her lap.

Alejandrina broke her reverie. "She has the purity of an angel."

"Who does?" Luz-divina demanded with a scowl.

"Your enemy. I see a virgin soul."

"No, you must be mistaken."

"No, my dear. It's you who's mistaken. You've stolen from a pure soul."

My maid shook her head in dizzying little half-circles. "No, no, she's a *puta*. She's filthy."

Alejandrina looked only more serene, more transcendent, more visionary when she said, "Hers is a purity that can never be soiled. As eternal as the Holy Ghost—never."

And that's when an enraged Luz-d decided that this Alejandrina was a charlatan and a thief. She shot up as swiftly as can be expected given her girth and the mushiness of the sofa, and made to leave, but the harbinger called her back. "It's a hundred dollars."

"You ought to be ashamed of yourself," she spat, throwing a pile of wrinkled, sweaty cash at the oracle. Alejandrina stared silently, her glowing chestnut gaze a whirlpool of intimidating wisdom and pity. Trembling, Luz-d found her way out to the street, where the daylight hurt her eyes and made her squint. She thought of me once more, now from a new angle: I was still a defiled whore, but totally unashamed, who regarded herself as beyond reproach, a paragon of virtue. Now Lu-di finally saw me clearly. The Vaseline had been wiped off the lens of her mind and she saw how I had willfully chosen my life, deliberately turned my back on G-d, *decided* to be a whore despite every advantage. Beautiful, rich, Northern, educated—my shame was a triple-sin because it should have been otherwise. She would show me.

Though it wasn't her day to clean the librarian's place, she went anyway, confident that I would be at work. I was, so she violated the sanctuary whose locks had not yet been changed, doubtlessly intending to steal (back) the DVD archive. No, Lulu, no. Did you underestimate me yet again? Could you actually have believed that I would be careless enough to leave them within the radius of your slinking paws? No, little Margarita mixer, I wasn't. Your old shoebox and all its astoundingly complex contents sat smirking in my Society foot locker, where I also kept a bottle of aspirin (for stress headaches), my pro-biotic supplements (for when the deli was out of plain yogurt), a comb, and spare lipstick. You were frustrated again.

The box, she knew, was a shared Achilles' heel between the men and myself. Luz-divina looked searchingly around the sparse embellishments of my home, frantically and with a parched mouth, trying to understand how to bring the psychic's prophecy to fruition. Had she understood the value of the tapestry, she would have stolen or destroyed it, but luckily my tastes run to the austere, so it escaped notice. Segismundo then whimpered, his delicate sense of correctness disturbed by her agitated mood. Yes, man's best friend. She would remove my only solace, my sole soul mate, my partner in life's fickle scenes. Finally acting as the murderer who had inhabited her poisoned heart all along, divine Lulu excused herself, scurried down to the nearest supermarket, and slipped in again, unnoticed by the on-duty building staff (Alvaro was off), and the other elevator riders, accustomed as they were to the comings and goings of washed-out domestic help.

Humming to herself, hands shaking, she prepared a gooey bowl of the delectable organic dog food I special-ordered from California. It probably was more expensive ounce-for-ounce than anything she ever ate. Doomed Segismundo, whose puppyhood had been spent as a kennel slave, rectum assailed by hot peppers, beaten for incomprehensible infractions, raced senselessly to exhaustion, then abandoned, now would feel momentary bliss at an unscheduled feeding. What a treat! He approached her bloated ankles, tail wagging furiously as she stirred in the white powder, careful that it should blend in to the sumptuous gravy. As she stooped to set the bowl down in front of him, my sweet doll licked her face in gratitude.

And can you believe she'd forgotten about the perpetually seeing eye she'd planted there herself?

That same afternoon, she began her long trip home.

Upon slow-motion playback, I called Alvaro and invited him over for a little glass of tequila. It was his day off, so it would take him a while to arrive, though he went to great pains to make it known that the pleasure was all his. I feared that he would bring some digestion-destroying courtesy snacks, so I made sure to tell him to only get some tomato juice for the chaser. I would take care of the rest. Eyes reddened with mourning, I steadfastly set about making a fresh guacamole and crudités platter. It was hard not to think about the canine corpse on ice in my bathtub, but I had to get into character for Alvaro, and fussing with it like a mortician would only worsen my mood.

By the time the doorbell rang, I was composed and smiling, dry-eyed and rouge-cheeked. After we had made ourselves comfortable (especially him, whose comfort lay in my thigh-high stockings and calfskin pumps), I lightly dropped this: "Listen, Luz-divina left me a note saying that she had to return to Mexico for a little while. She wanted me to send her last day's pay there, but I guess she was in such a hurry, she forgot to leave her address!" I forced myself to giggle.

He sat up in alarm. "What? Did I hear you right?"

I slowly repeated it all, this time in Spanish, not because his English wasn't perfect, but to remind him to relax. He indicated that this was news to him. He couldn't believe she would depart without telling him first. "Hand me my cell," he demanded curtly.

I obeyed, calmly waiting to see what he would find out. I was curious myself, had she gone home, or was she silly enough to risk hanging around here? He called Lupe, the roommate I hadn't met, and listened with knitted brow. He swiftly hung up, then turned to me. "Ximena, I'm sorry, but this is a family crisis. She's gone, with most of her things, and even her roommates don't really understand. She left a note that only said she had gone back to her village…our village, I have family there, too. I have to go check this out."

I assured him I understood, even helping him to get dressed. As he stood tucking in his shirt, I reminded him, "So, I still need her address, you know?" He wrote it from memory on the first blank page in my gilded notebook.

"By the way," he asked from the doorway, "where's the dog?"

"Oh, my friend borrowed him for protection. Her house was broken into."

"Really? But I thought greyhounds really weren't guard dogs."

"You're right. They aren't, but he was all I had. Anyway, all she needs is a placebo." He was all I had.

Servants, be obedient to them that are your masters according to the flesh, with fear and trembling, in singleness of heart, as unto Christ; not with eyeservice, as men-pleasers; but as the servants of Christ, doing the will of God from the heart.

EPH. VI. 5, 6.

Segismundo's cremation was too personal an event to describe here. Anyway, it has nothing to do with this story.

He was handed back to me in a small urn.

Still Collecting & Cataloging at the Society, and still spritzing *Pleasure* in a stupor, my finances were still anemic, at best. I needed a cash cushion upon which to rest until I could wrench Luz-divina's earnings away from her. They were, in fact, mine. Think about it: *my* carefully cultivated relationships, *my* custom-made costumes, *my* dwelling, and *my* rolling chrome bar had made her a six-digit nest egg. Invested wisely, it could be worth even more. She, of course, was too rough around the edges to invest wisely in anything, but I hoped it would never go that far.

The only possession that could be fruitfully liquidated was my tapestry. I had received it as a very special gift from my thesis advisor (completely inappropriate, I know) during my junior year abroad in Madrid. A distinguished man, many years my senior, his vast inherited wealth had freed him up to earn multiple doctorates in arcane subjects, to collect art of exceptional quality, and to make these kinds of extravagant gifts to whomever he chose. I suppose it was his own customized version of philanthropy. (He also happened to have other remarkably eccentric tastes, but that's a whole other book.)

I rummaged through the small clear drawers of my desk to find the business card of an independent curator who had done a wonderful job at the Society, before I had come to work there, with an exhibition on the Spanish Netherlands. I recall it being well-ordered, creative, and enlightening. Though we had never met, this Mr. Paul Lewis had inspired awe in Dr. González-Feinmann, my superior. I had heard he ran a small art dealership, specializing in Spanish colonial things. Loathe as I was to part with my favorite object, it felt like nothing compared to saying farewell to my greyhound, to say nothing of losing Pedro's companionship. In her blundering way, corpulent Lululu had already stripped me of quite a lot.

Over the phone, this Mr. Paul Lewis sounded pleasant enough. He asked me to come by in an hour. I was a little taken aback by the immediacy of it all, but shouldn't have been surprised. The Society is a wonderful calling card. I hurriedly changed into a sober suit and pumps, pinned my hair into a twist, and made my lips red. In these instances, it's always better to look like a terrifically preserved older woman than like an actual youthful one. The ten year padding made me feel ready to do business. Carefully rolling the tapestry between layers of white tissue paper, gently setting it into its chocolate leather folio, and gingerly sealing it under the X that my thesis advisor had thoughtfully had embossed on the flap, I took it out for a cab ride uptown.

Mr. Lewis' gallery was suitably plush to inspire confidence. Double-glazed windows muffled the

Madison Avenue traffic noise, while thin modernist furnishings directed the eye to some hauntingly live Mesoamerican masks on pedestals. He must have kept the really good stuff off-site in a warehouse. He greeted me with a too-tonic handshake to go with his faint smile. I thought I might have seen his left eyebrow shoot up as I walked toward him. He wasn't at all what I had pictured: grey beard, platinum cufflinks. No, rather he was young, about exactly my chronological age, wearing a hip suit and ankle boots with sporty soles. He put on a pair of glasses, in a blue titanium frame, to inspect the tapestry. "And, you have papers for this?"

"Yes, right here." I handed him the dossier.

"Mm'hmm." He looked them over knowingly, nodding. He barely could mask his surprise at the quality of the piece.

We talked pricing. He was realistic; it all sounded about right. "Listen, Mr. Lewis," I sat forward in my chair, so that he could imagine he felt the heat rising off my knees, "I need to raise some money just now, but I expect to," I paused, "come into a sizeable inheritance soon, so I'd like the option of buying this back from you before you show it to any of your clients. Could we arrange something like that?"

He indicated that he understood all too clearly— here there was a little smirk that could have meant any number of things—and we discussed a sizeable loan. It obviously wasn't the first time he'd functioned like a high-end pawn shop. So, I hocked a piece of my heart. Feeling like a mother leaving the orphanage without her child, I gave him my contact information, and collected my clutch to go. He thanked me for choosing him for this important transaction, wished me well, and told me, as he squeezed my hand a second time, "When you called, I had no idea you would be so young and," he paused, "charming."

"We'll see each other soon, I hope." I had too many important matters clamoring for my attention to attend to what could have been a gratifying and lucrative affair. I was forced to pass. Score another one for the L team!

Pocket money thus augmented, I undertook the unseemly task of asking Dr. González-Feinmann for a leave of absence. Unable to produce a medical note (and regardless, unwilling to tempt Fate with a faked illness), I fed him a vague story about attending to the estate of my deceased parents. I would need to meet with lawyers and the like in person, and given Chilean bureaucracy, there was no telling when I would be back. I winced inwardly as I openly lied to the honest, learned man who had given me the best career opportunity of my life. I chastised myself for this loss of control, and promised myself that I would never be in such a diminished position again. To my relief, he asked for no elaboration, and agreed to let me go under the condition that my leave be unpaid. The Society would need to hire a temporary Cataloger to deal with their backlog while I was away, and couldn't afford to pay us both. I gratefully accepted and promised to e-mail from Santiago with an estimated return date as soon as I had one.

Running my fingertips along the edges of my desk one last time before diving into the unheated pool of unpaid leave, it occurred to me that I would be needing good reading for my trip—something stimulating and challenging, not the soft-core sleeping pills they sell as literature in the stores. Browsing the spines stacked in my In-Progress pile, one title caught my eye because it contained the name of the very valley where I would be pursuing justice during my vacation. *The Paradise Garden Murals of Malinalco: utopia and empire in sixteenth-century Mexico* promised to be a juicy read! Since it had yet to be cataloged, the volume lived in that no-man's-land where no scholars yet knew of its existence, so none could be clamoring for it.

Unusually home in the middle of the day, I gobbled green seedless grapes and parroted the manufactured story all over again to Lindsay over the phone. She saw this as cause for jubilation, citing *closure* again as a premium value. Little did she know, I was actually going to Mexico, for *rupture*. The important thing was that she didn't worry about my absence, and didn't think anything strange was going on. Lindsay thinking I was normal had come to be my only solace during that turbulent period, and I couldn't cope with jeopardizing that. I felt like I would unravel if my only remaining best friend saw me as a penniless pervert.

Then I packed a bag of warm weather clothing, ample sunscreen and dietary supplements. I had never been to Mexico at all before—forget about the Aztec capital of Malinalco.

I set up camp for a few days at the Hotel Jardín Real to acclimate myself to Mexico City. What with her stunted legal status and all, I figured that it would take Lu-di quite some time to make it back to home's sweet bosom. I had a vivid mental picture of her leaving from Port Authority on a Greyhound bus to the Texas border, then paying a coyote in damp wads of cash to take her back across the border, where she would then hitchhike back to her mystical valley. (I couldn't have been more wrong, it turns out. Later, during de-briefing, Lu-di explained, I thought somewhat arrogantly, that she had entered and left the supermax facility that is America on her cousin Rosalba's passport. Rosalba actually did possess a kind of diminished work visa, for the domestic staff of diplomats, and therefore was not *persona non grata* in our land. Remember that this Rosalba had briefly worked for me before having had to relinquish her coveted spot. I had even met her once, when I returned home early from work with a sore throat, and she had been running late. I tell you, she was considerably sweeter of feature and more graceful in person than her cousin, but one can forgive Immigration for playing the fool. In the documents Luz-D showed me, it became clear that Rosalba was terribly unphotogenic; and the two could have passed for twins.)

Killing hours like so many mosquitoes, I visited their legendary museum, ate their atrocious food, and swam in their courtyard pool, where vines climbed the pink stucco walls like prison escapees, and even the plush towels wore inmate's stripes. The high altitude boosted the sun's already maddening force, so that by the third day, I had a real tan, the kind worn by light-hearted vacationers. It was on that third day that I sat absorbed in the purloined book, sipping an iced coffee from a red striped straw. Iridescent hummingbirds lunched at a feeder; orange butterflies sucked at the trough of some blossoms. According to the authoress, Malinalco was famed for its monolithic Aztec temples, but also had hidden astounding sixteenth-century frescoes beneath whitewash until the 1970's. Snowy egrets, wild-eyed rabbits, and pomegranate imagery abounded.

As anyone could have predicted by now, a well-dressed man approached. "May I?" he asked, indicating the lounger next to mine. I nodded haughtily to indicate he could sit, but that I reserved the right to ask him to stand again at any moment. He sat at the foot of the lounger, in the uncomfortable pose of a fully dressed person. He introduced himself, extended a well-manicured hand, and complimented my language skills. "Do you like Mexican food?"

"May I be honest with you, sir?" Of course I could be honest with him. One can always be honest with strangers. It's intimates to whom one has to lie. "I don't care for it at all."

He beamed. "That's just what I thought, Miss. It's Miss, isn't it?"

I smiled an of-course smile.

His grin broadened to an almost comical degree. "Then allow me take you out for a dinner you will never forget for all your life, even after you return to your country."

"Mexican food?" He was presentable and amiable enough, but I would not spend my evening politely sampling tamales and regional cheeses.

"No, dear. Food you've never had. Cuisine with no name, from before the Conquest." Intrigued, I agreed to meet him in the lobby in three hours. Another liberating aspect of masochism is that it makes you pretty fearless. I seldom fear anything bad happening to me mainly because I have survived so many truly horrible acts. And even enjoyed them. But no, my instincts told me he was harmless.

We binged on foods that had never before crossed my palate: corn fungus, bitter greens, crunchy worms, ant caviar. I'll spare you the tedious verbal gymnastics that led to his generous offer. I'm always in favor of moving the story right along. According to him, many generations of his family had died, leaving him solely in charge of the seventeenth-century hacienda they had once used for cattle, but that had gradually been converted into an art warehouse and summer resting place. It happened to lie midway between Cuernavaca and Malinalco, and was sitting dormant save for a couple of groundskeepers, their wives, children, dogs, and the field mice. He was certain I would be happier and more comfortable there than in any of the sub-standard and overpriced accommodation in Malinalco, a town he assured me was singularly unequipped for travelers, because of, or anyway contributing to, the gross under-rating of its cultural heritage. He could scarcely think of anyone who would more deeply appreciate the library of Spanish history and literature his grandfather had accumulated, or the altar frescoes in the family chapel. To make it impossible for me to say no, he would even lend me a car and driver for the duration of my stay. I needn't worry about personal security, not even about amorous advances—he laughed—as he himself would be in Monterrey on business. He chuckled again, with the smug satisfaction that comes with high-end magnanimity. Of course, I protested and demurred, always maintaining a vague attitude about why I was even visiting Malinalco, but by the time the pumpkin *flan* and molten *cajeta* were between us, I had arranged a time for his driver to pick me up the following day.

The air cleaned itself up as we left the periphery of the Capital. The kind stranger's driver was a punctual and polite man in a sport shirt and jeans clinging almost lewdly to an overly muscular physique. I sat in the back, lost in my own thoughts, while he sped recklessly through the arid landscape in our glossy red sedan. Watching the evenly paved road slide beneath us, and the plant life slide past us, I reflected on how detached I felt from my mission. In fact, it was a classic vendetta, yet I wasn't crazed with hatred or anger. I'd read so many stories about vendetta, but I'd never before been the protagonist of one. It felt sickening and invigorating at the same time, like racing motorcycles or having hot wax poured on your most delicate patches of skin. I fervently hoped my antagonist had made it home safe and sound, so that I would find her there to detain for a talk. She and I had communicated in so many ways over the past few months—we'd exchanged money and confidences; I'd made love to her cousin and sat in her chair—but we'd yet to meet. We were clearly long overdue for a good, long talk.

The stranger's house was as splendid as described. A U-shaped corridor of richly decorated rooms surrounded a garden courtyard, then a row of stables adjoining the servants' quarters lined a road leading to the chapel. My bedroom was adorned with faded blue and gold paisley wallpaper, a darkly polished four-poster bed, and oil paintings of ancestors. A white ceramic pitcher held some charming wildflowers. It was cozy in an outdated nunnery sort of way, though the desolation of the grounds lent a correctional quality, I thought.

I made myself at home with a hot bath and hot snack brought in by one of the tiniest adult women I have ever seen. She was the cook during the off-season. When the estate was in use, the staff population swelled, and she became the real cook's assistant. She went home to Oaxaca twice a year, for Day of the Dead and Christmas, and hoped I would enjoy her Oaxaca style cooking. I swear she curtsied on her way out, reminding me to leave the tray outside my door when I was done with it.

I summoned the driver, who was named Angél, with the intention of asking him to drive me to Luz-divina's address in Malinalco, but as I waited for him, it dawned on me that she would likely be terribly unwilling to talk with me. The more I thought about it, the less I could picture her inviting me in for a tête-à-tête, or even accompanying me somewhere else to chat in privacy. No, indeed there would be an embarrassing scene, of the sort I had spent my entire life trying to avoid. I doubted that Lulu herself would become violent, but one never did know about her relatives and neighbors. Angél knocked on my door.

I let him in, sat him down, and asked him if he would run an important errand for me. I would more than adequately recompense him for his time, of course. (My budget had increased tremendously since discovering I would have no hotel, car, or food expenses. I hadn't previously thought of hiring personal security, but now that Angél had floated into my life, I understood that he was that, too.) I gave him Luz-divina's name, address, and a physical description that probably could have fit two-thirds of the women in her neighborhood. I explained to him that she was a distant, very distant, relative of mine, we had quarreled, and I had come all the way from Nueva York to make peace with her. She was a feisty woman who took after a notoriously crazy common ancestor of ours, what can you do? I instructed him to bring her back here for dinner. Knowing her and her stubborn ways (and history of insanity—she had spent time in a mental hospital in my country), she might well resist coming. If that turned out to be the case, and he had to force her into the car, I would pay him a bonus. I knew how difficult she could be, and I wouldn't be stingy about that. Angél, who had changed into a new sport shirt, looked skeptical, reluctant at first, but ultimately shrugged and agreed. He would try his best. We set a double-tiered price system.

His dust clouds still hanging over the driveway, I walked over to the kitchen to tell the cook we would be having a special guest. Perhaps she could prepare something extra? No problem. She said it was the same effort cooking for two as for one. Their kitchen was a delightfully analog affair, with stone mortars, copper pots, and a wood-burning oven that all looked like part of a museum display. It smelled intense, like smoked leather and a fresh-cut lawn.

Then I quieted my jangling nerves with a book. As I read, the peripheral vision of my mind caught glimpses, again and again, of various worst-case scenarios. She could have not returned home, but instead was spending my money in another American city. I flashed on a picture of her smoking a cigar in Chicago. She could have returned to Mexico, but not to her hometown. I flashed on her gorging herself on raw seafood in a '60's-looking Acapulco resort. She could be using my money to build a duplex home in a lovely town she had always favored, near a monastery and a butterfly migratory resting forest. Alternately, she could have returned home, as she had reported to her roommates, but just not be *at home* when Angél alighted. That would be a drag. I nervously flipped pages, barely scanning the text. Luckily, the utopian paradise garden murals of Malinalco took a good picture, so my eyes found a resting place.

Dust clouds again in the driveway. I walked out to the portico just as Angél was hopping out from behind the wheel. I stopped at the step and looked out anxiously as he walked around to the passenger's side, gallantly opened the door, and helped a stout, disheveled figure to disembark. Yes, it had to be her. Though we had never met, I recognized the petty cunning, bad tailoring, faulty logic, and misguided entitlement that had to be my maid. Angél led her by the arm, not so gently, to where I stood. Depositing her at the top of the stairs, he wordlessly turned and walked back to the cherry red car, which he immediately started to wipe down with a rag. Stunned, surprised, scared—her face transmitted them all. I told her to follow me inside. She did, like a robot, into the side sitting room. Indicating a wine velvet armchair for her, I left her there to stew in her own incomprehension and powerlessness, as I put together a tray of cold beer and frosty mugs I had spotted in the industrial-size fridge. The cook stopped me on my way out to add a bowl of guacamole, a floppy stack of corn tortillas, and a bowl of halved limes. The tray was heavy; I wobbled a little bringing it in to Luz-divina. She uttered not a word as I opened a bottle, and poured it slowly enough to avoid foam overflow. I handed it to her, then did the same for myself, excruciatingly slowly, striptease pace. One thing her face didn't indicate was bewilderment. She clearly knew exactly who I was, if not *what* I was. Hers was the distant, but sure recognition normal people reserve for film stars. She had, after all, seen me in many movies. All my suspicions were vindicated in all the instants she didn't cry out, "But, who are you?"

I'm not normally a beer drinker, but that one tasted exquisite to me. I squeezed in some extra lime for vitamin C. If she was going to play the mute, I would start. "How are you, Luz-divina? Well?"

She blinked too rapidly, like a hostage in an internet broadcast. "I didn't know you spoke Spanish."

"There's a lot about me you don't know. We haven't yet met. I'm Ximena. It's a pleasure to finally meet you." I extended my hand to shake hers, but it remained limply flopped in her over-padded lap. Well, I could understand that. I continued, "I'm here because I think we need to talk. There have been a lot of misunderstandings between us, haven't there?"

She nodded and squeaked.

"But let's not get into that right now. You must have had an exhausting day. Is this beer ok?"

Luz-divina's first-ever set of full sentences to me was this: "How did you get this beer in the summer? They only sell it at Christmas time. It's the best. You must have a huge freezer here." I can never forget that partially because once she broke her silence, she became a wellspring of torrential comments, and partially just because I was amazed that anyone would bother to stockpile beer for seven months. Maybe I shouldn't have taken them out, but then again the cook would have stopped me if the gentleman was saving them for a special occasion. The label did have poinsettia all over it.

Just then, the delicate little cook padded in to announce that dinner was ready. We followed her into the dining room, a vaulted-ceilinged affair with dark wood paneling, candelabras, and more ancestor portraits. Lu-di was awed, that much was obvious. Her jaw was slack and her eyes were shining. I noticed that the cook had changed into a proper uniform, doll-sized in her case, of the sort that my maid had never had to wear. It was a nice touch. The individual dishes were timidly announced: chicken *mole*, Oaxaca cheese, *jicama* salad, rice. And she retreated. A crystal decanter held some viscous-looking red wine. Again, I poured it out, watching Luz-d transparently rejoice in being waited on.

We dined mostly in lip-smacking silence, gulping our wine and complimenting the cooking. Over dessert of over-ripe mangoes and coffee, we resumed our meet-and-greet session. I asked about her family, and she gushed emotionally about the adorable little boy, the touchingly crippled little girl, and their absentee fathers. Speaking to her it became obvious that she recognized only two motifs, the Cute and the Pathetic, and prized above all a combination of the two. Ratcheting up those themes in a life that was devoid of the former and steeped in the latter became my tactical challenge. There was no way I was telling her my truth. She asked about my parents and siblings and I made up a sympathetic lie. Not only was my mother, in this version, a struggling widow, but my younger brother had died in a bicycle accident, and my older sister had wed a horrible man who had forced her to relocate to a distant and inaccessible suburb of...of...Minneapolis. (I thought that throwing in harsh winters would be particularly shocking to my interlocutor.) I indulged in a memory of a prematurely killed puppy that would have been a thinly veiled accusation to someone else, but was received by her as a painfully frank story.

It grew late, but I refrained from cutting to the chase. Now that I knew where she lived, as it were, I could proceed unhurriedly. So instead of speaking of the business that hovered between us like a miasma of biochemical weapon gas, I took her on a tour of the property. She barely glanced at the library, but was enthralled by the pool, a stubby box too short for laps and too shallow for diving, lined with yellow and blue ceramic tiles. I invited her over to swim the following morning. "But, I don't have a swimsuit," she said Pathetically.

"That's ok," I assured her Cutely, "you can borrow one from the cook." (Assuming the cook had one lying around that was ten sizes too big for her.)

"But, I don't know how to swim!" Now there was real anguish in her voice.

"That's ok," I double-assured her, "It's not deep. You can stand in it."

Her face lit up with a fabulous idea. "Can I bring my kids?"

"Sure!" I said brightly, then switched to Pathetic. "I love kids. I've always wanted some of my own, but I can't have any."

"Why not?" She certainly was nosy.

"Because, Luz-divina, I just can't. My body."

We agreed that Angél would pick them up at an appointed hour and deposit them here for frolicking. I watched her depart with disgust. I wasn't sure what disgusted me more: her frank self-servingness, her misguided trust in me, her lack of apology for all the damage she'd wrought, or her imminent descent into pure humiliation. In short, once I'd met her, I hated everything about her so fully that my hate even encompassed her ignorance of that same hate. I hated her so completely that I no longer hated her *because* she had abused my largesse, unlawfully placed me under surveillance, severed my five most meaningful human relationships, and profited from them, but rather it came to seem that doing all that was perfectly consistent with her human mission. She was born poor, ugly, and inept, and the days of her life ticked by only so that she better embody poverty (of luck and spirit), ugliness, and ineptitude. I relished and didn't relish seeing her again in the morning, the way one anticipates and yet doesn't anticipate the next stinging blow against the buttocks.

The hacienda had wireless internet, thank god. I was coming to appreciate, in absentia, the kind stranger more and more. He was a gracious host and a fine judge of character. I made an executive decision that if he changed his mind and visited, I would sleep with him. I had a hunch, wandering through his rooms, that we were into some of the same things. My inbox read as an unreal, white-washed version of reality, devoid of vendetta, debt, class warfare, and commodified violence. (To get news of those things, I'd have to have written to myself.) From Lindsay:

hi X!
i don't know if you're reading your mail in chile, so if you're not, don't worry about it...but if you are...
i hope everything is progressing swimmingly with your parents' estate, and that it's not too hard for you.

these situations can be very emotional, and i want you know i'm here to talk!

work is crazy. i'm soooo busy and going out of my mind with this public health presentation. i did, though, meet a very HANDSOME lawyer in the cafeteria. he got my NUMBER! so, i will keep you posted...hopefully, i will have some juicy stories by the time you get back.

big hug,
linz
p.s. latest acquisition for my euro-slogan tee collection: NIENTE RACISMO!

From Dr. González-Feinmann:

Dear Ximena,
Just sending salutations from the library, where your help is missed. We are lost without you.

Wishing you the best of luck in the land of Neruda,
Dr. González-Feinmann

From Alvaro [via phone]:

hi beautiful
things here are dull

i miss you a lot
call me when you get back, ok?

a.

The sun shone in glittering sheets of lemon satin the morning Luz-divina's clan decamped to my erstwhile hacienda. Bracing myself against whatever virulent strain of evil I'd contracted from her, I glanced back and forth between the dueling azures of cloudless sky and chlorinated pool water. I had meanwhile dredged up a threadbare one-piece (thank god not a bikini) from one of the guest room closets that was stretched out enough and missing enough elastic to approximate a good fit for my deformed friend. It was the faded red of an overused child's rubber ball. I debated whether I should get into my suit as well, to show camaraderie and a willingness to get wet with her gimpy kids, but I thought better of it. The last time I'd worn a bathing suit in a public place, a silver-haired woman in blue glasses had handed me the business card of her body part modeling agency. Lulu would not be able to cope.

The children spilled out of the car accompanied by a soundtrack of such innocence—giggles, Mommy, Mommy, pudgy hand claps—that for a split second, flashing somewhere in that interstice between sensation and cognition, I almost turned back down the road to which their mother had lead me with her first treacherous act. The double spontaneous orphan in me melted, crystallizing into the warm-hearted potential mother who would spare Lulu for the sake of her little family, then melted again and crystallized for good into the naked, defenseless woman she had robbed of her scant wealth and frayed dignity. She had never taken pity on me; why should I extend the courtesy to her?

With the assistance of Angél and the Oaxacan cook, we frolicked in the sun together, devoured home made fruit sorbets, played frisbee. Luz-d and her son and daughter splashed in the pool like sparrows in a birdie bath. "Ximena," she called to me without getting out of the water, "why don't you come in, too? The temperature is perfect!"

"I would," I sadly intoned, "but I'm far too pale. I've never been able to tolerate the sun." I adjusted my wide-brimmed hat for emphasis.

"Mommy," the little girl *sotto voce*'d at high volume, "she's like Luisito, the albino. You know him?" Luz-d shushed her, and slapped her arm a little roughly, I thought, for disciplining a disabled little girl, and hypocritically, too, considering how fundamentally rude she was herself.

"Oh yes, I understand," Lulu said, addressing herself to me, "That's very unfortunate."

"It is," I agreed, "I've missed out on a lot of fun on account of my skin, especially when I was Mariluz' age."

Nodding, she threw in, somewhat gratuitously, "I'm allergic to peanuts. If I eat even one, my throat closes up like a turtle." Though I couldn't quite make the turtle image work, I was a little surprised that she knew about her allergy and was still alive. That fact alone indicated that she must have had decent medical care in her childhood.

After they had toweled off, and were lolling on the lush grass, I indicated to Lulu that we should get rid of the kids to talk woman stuff. She seemed to like the chance to pretend for a little while that we were friends and she was engaging in a sophisticated social life with an albino librarian from Manhattan. The little tykes were coerced to trundle off to the kitchen to bake sugar cookies—from scratch!—with the cook. They grumbled less than I would've imagined. Maybe they really were starved for warm domestic scenes. Even the boy complied, maybe because having had no father had left him a bit effeminate.

Alone under a parasol at a wrought iron lawn table, I changed my countenance dramatically, not to a stern mood per se, but to one that indicated a serious discussion was to follow. Brows knit, I told her, "I'm not in the least angry with you."

"Why not?" she quite sensibly asked.

"Because those men were Bad. I never should have let them hit me in the first place. They were adulterers. They sinned and got what they deserved." She smiled and nodded with vigor and relief. I couldn't believe how readily she accepted this kind of bland, insipid thought gruel, but then again life had already taught me a thousand times over that you can only overestimate people; to underestimate humans is virtually impossible. Nodding furiously, hands clasped either in piety or desperation, Lulu said nothing, so I pushed on, "In a way I'm even glad you did what you did." [Am I going too far, I asked myself, am I risking everything with this kind of redemptive talk?] "It put an end to my abuse. For that, I'm grateful." [I held my breath, just to see if she had seen through my crudely rendered act.]

Taking, I guess, my breath holding as a Pathetic and maybe even Cute need of affirmation, Luz-divina actually grabbed my hand. And held it firmly. "Ximena," she warbled, "you're most welcome. You can heal now. All that's behind you." I could see that her lifetime of television talk show viewing had not gone wasted. I exhaled loudly, my shoulders jerking. It was astounding to me that she was making no move whatsoever to apologize, and didn't even allude to the money. Mark that as the moment I understood just what a piece of work my maid really was. As per my training, I would play along, follow the scent of delusion as far down the street as it would lead.

"Thank you," I concluded, with a tone that said, Good, that's over. Now let's talk turkey. "You see, I've been thinking…about your smart idea…"

"Yes?" She perked up. Unaccustomed as she was to praise, it made her sit up straighter.

"Well," I lowered my voice to draw her puffy lumpen face closer to my chiseled and unblemished one. Little birds twittered in the nearby trees with a malicious joy. "I thought it was really good the way you interacted with those disgusting men. You showed them justice and pity at the same time." She nodded gravely, indicating that my speech was neither too baroque nor too embarrassing for her. It egged me on. "Frankly though, they deserved worse. Much worse."

"Much worse?" she repeated like an imbecile.

"Yes. They're all extremely rich, yet they never gave me anything. Not so much as a gold bracelet." Lulu's expression was rapt, that of a little girl glimpsing the beckoning forest to which she had been denied entry in absolute. "Luz-divina, I tell you, they are so miserly, you can't believe it! Not a dinner out. The occasional box of Dunkin' Donuts for all that abuse."

"Really?" She didn't know what to think.

"And let's not forget their wives. What haven't they put those poor women through? Ultimately, I don't think your modest requests made even a dent in their morals." This last bit, I delivered with the calm triumph of a person setting a wreath down upon a coffin.

"How did you know about that, anyway?"

I waved my hand to indicate how off-topic this was. "I know a lot of things. I'm an information professional and I speak languages. Don't forget I have all the movies." [I called them movies because I thought she would have been calling them movies to herself the whole time.]

Her eyes twitched laterally in a REM-like motion as she mulled that over. After what seemed like a full minute, she came out with, "But haven't you destroyed them?"

It then took me a minute in turn to realize she was considering my shame. The poor idiot had really never grasped anything about it or me. "I wanted to. Believe me, I wanted to more than anything in the world. However, it's my only weapon against them. Without the movies, I am defenseless." I almost laughed at my own ridiculous logic, but she was serious as surgery.

"And?" Lulu asked cagily. Her greed was one step behind her sluggish mind, or maybe she was understandably stunned by our meeting.

"Can I get you another refreshment?" I cut in, gesturing at her empty soda glass. I didn't want her refined sugar addiction coming between us.

"No, I'm fine," she said hurriedly. She was dying to know what I'd propose and why, after all, I was in the State of Mexico.

"And. And I believe we could do it all again for a much larger sum." Her eyes widened hideously. "They can afford it. And, I hadn't thought of this before, but now that you've brought it all into the light, I'd like a gift, too. To pay for all the therapy I'm going to need. They made me a little sick." I looked down in post-trauma.

"I see," she said hesitantly, "but what does that have to do with me?"

"Don't worry, I'm not asking for your money back. That's between you and them. You earned that. I want to go halves on the new money."

"Why? Why don't you do it alone?"

"Because they obviously know where I live and everything about me. They might resist. They're already used to controlling me. You're the neutral stranger, and they already respect you. They'll give you again more of what they gave you before."

"How do you know they won't resist me, too?" So she did have a smidgen of common sense.

"Because, Luz-divina, they have too much to lose. They're afraid of you. They have no idea who you know, or how far you'll go. What if you gave the movies to their wives or bosses? If you promise this is the end, they'll deliver. I know them."

"And we split it?"

"Yes."

"And I keep the first bit?"

"Yes."

"But, why can't I do it from here, on the internet?"

"Because if one of them refuses, you'll have to visit him in person."

"Let me think, Ximena. I'll have a definite answer for you tomorrow. I have to go to church and pray for an answer."

Yeah, you do that.

I availed myself of Malinalco's superb Aztec ruins while the tumor on my heart prayed to her savior. The weather was clear and fine. Strolling at my leisure, I shooed away the haranguing would-be guides in favor of solitude. It was breathtaking. One forgets how grandiose, and inspiring, and monolithic monoliths really are until one is standing at the foot of one, half-blinded by the sun and dazzled by the heavens, neck craned all the way the back to see it in its entirety. The serpents, the eagles, they were all in place, imposing their regal eternal gazes on a valley that had sunk lower than was ever intended. The humans in the town below had been dealt a mean deal by the world order; nothing they did in this lifetime would boost their status in this society or any other. The only question remaining open to them was whether to stay at the bottom here or seek the wealthier bottom in the North.

Next, I toured the paradise garden murals from the book. I was the only person at the more obscure site. My footfalls echoed and my shadows flickered alone. It was truly splendid.

By the time I'd returned to the house, borne by Angél, Luz-divina, greedy, naïve, and predictable as a bunny, had already come calling and was waiting for me in a plush armchair. I guess she prayed fast. And her God must have been an idiot, as she was ready to accept my offer. [Just an aside:

Hypothetically now, Reader, I ask you, if *you* had abused someone's openhandedness, spied on her, recorded her in the most compromising of positions, blackmailed her lovers, robbed her of her income, fled the country, and *then,* enjoying the fruits of your crime in the privacy of your ancestral home, *she* showed up across international boundaries, displaying an uncanny ability to discover your address, setting up temporary residence in an aristocratic ranch, and asked you to *go back with her,* would you? Would you not find it threatening or suspicious?] Luz-divina agreed. It was then that she shared with me the convenience of Rosalba's passport and visa, and even, I kid you not, produced a printed schedule of Mexicana Airlines flights.

Like a pretend sleepwalker, I followed her into the agreement that we would leave the day after tomorrow, on a non-stop from the Federal District to JFK. No cajoling necessary. We trusted each other, it appeared, like two high-wire walkers in the same circus. We parted a little breathlessly, she eager to pack for her next trip to New York, me trepidatious of all that lay ahead. I don't fool myself about life's essentially sadistic nature—if stage one had been easy, stage two would have to be doubly arduous. I couldn't imagine the exact flavor of what it would be like having Luz-d back in New York with me, only that it would taste disgusting.

I paced the paneled halls, that night, of the hacienda. The little gears in my mind clicked savagely. To dull them, I jotted a game plan in my gilt notebook.

```
       Comportment Upon Return to the
                  Cloister:
        Do not inform the Society of my
                  return.
     Do not call Lindsay.  If I run into
      Lindsay, say that I just got back
                  that day.
       Re-ingratiate myself with Alvaro.
     Correctly archive the surveillance
            discs.  Add meta-data.
                Get the money.
```

My last night there was spent reclining on my left side, linen handkerchief folded under my cheek, crying until the thing was soaked. All my dreams and intentions of a copasetic life were being shattered anew every minute I spent on un-doing Luz-divina's gross deeds. I felt compromised just knowing her, and debased to be on the same team.

But packing, the next morning, the few belongings I had scattered in my Mexican rooms, was a pleasure. My stay had been short, sweet, and effective. Nightmare daydreams of pursuing the tubby housecleaner across cactus fields and over volcanoes, while she thwarted and evaded me, days turning into weeks and even months…those never materialized. The docile little lamb was allowing me to fold my little shirts into a suitcase after only a short vacation. Here was the case that idiots long to see: stupidity as an adjunct of the Good. After months of careful scheming and clever risk-taking, Luz-divina had finally collapsed into the sweet atrophy of guilelessness.

I bid my mental goodbye to the kind landholder. In general, I was and am much more of a taker than a giver. However, I was so moved by the stranger's generosity that I uncharacteristically lost my head and impulsively left the utopian book on the table in the main dining room as a token of gratitude.

Angél performed his last act of mercy in dropping us off at the airport. I felt like I was traveling with a terrorist, but Luz-d's bland demeanor and forgettable face raised no concerns with anyone. She breezed right through all checkpoints with Rosalba's paperwork, even pausing at Passport Control to shoot me an arch glance. I smiled at her benignly, my gaze focused slightly above her head, to give the impression, were anyone watching, of I Can't Help It If They Like Me.

At Check-In, Irony had her way with the discovery that Rosalba was a Platinum Member of that airline's bonus miles program. Five minutes after taking a seat in the waiting area with a newspaper, I had to clench my jaw as my toilet scrubber, or rather her predecessor, was summoned by public address to the counter to be upgraded to First Class. Setting down her celebrity tabloid, she waddled to her reward with such determined delight that, for a second, my desire to liberate the money from its incarceration in her care was outweighed by a perversely gripping desire to turn her in to the U.S. Immigration authorities. I would watch impassively, and maybe become moist in the crotch, as three uniformed officers, one a buxom female in ill-fitting pants, surrounded her, and guided her by one spongy forearm into a search room.

But no, I'd been thwarted by too many forces, too many times, to thwart myself.

Seated with seatbelt fastened and tray table set in an upright position, I watched the earth fall away from me, and the pyramids of Teotihuacán recede like porcelain figurines glimpsed from a moving car through someone's bedroom window. By the time the clouds had come level with the windows, I was dozing and lightly drooling. A jarring sensation at my elbow turned out to be none other than Luz-divina, my faithful maidservant, bearing a plastic flute of champagne and fresh baked chocolate chip cookie. I thanked her and watched her trundle back down the aisle, promptly flushing the drink down the toilet and crushing the biscuit underfoot. It wasn't me who needed First Class charity.

For the sake of brevity, I'll skip the slumber party scenes that unfolded in my corner of The Cloister upon our return. I've never had a sister, so it is not for me to say that the stilted chatter, steamed bathroom mirrors, and awkward dinners weren't just like real sisterhood, but I suspect not. It was closer to having a cellmate in a women's correctional institution (as I was to see) or a bunkmate in a loony bin.

She slept in shorts on an ad-hoc bedroll on the living room floor. Strangely, surprisingly, she required no coercion to stay at my place, instead of the vermin pit in the Bronx. I would've thought she would have wanted to stay with her own friends, but she apparently didn't even want to call them. So, thanks to long-simmering animosities, and location, location, location (The Cloister did have marvelous views), I had Luz-divina all to myself.

Apparently ashamed and guilty, or maybe not guilty, just ashamed (Lulu's morals reminded me very much of what they teach about the Japanese in undergraduate anthropology courses), she was hell-bent on avoiding Alvaro, insisting that her cousin not know she was back. In that way, we were alike, each preferring to do her dirty work away from the prying eyes of community. However, while I successfully was managing to avoid Lindsay, the Society, and the perfume spritzing agency, Lulu was not as lucky. I decided to undermine her wishes, not according to any special plan, but as a matter of principle. Once I had decided that her aims were antithetical to my well-being, I made it a flat policy to thwart them. So, claiming to go out for a run, an activity in which I was sure she would never want to participate, I slipped out our first night together to the building's storage room, where between crates of unused furniture and stacks of bicycles, I hurriedly copulated with a standing and uniformed Alvaro, then whispered into his graceful ear a cobbled-together report of Luz-divina having snuck back into the country. Out of the goodness of my heart, I was letting her stay with me until she had sorted out some problems with the Belgians, her former employees. I'd no idea why she didn't want to see her cousin and friends, but it was none of my business. I could only respect her wishes. He seemed a little stunned, but not overly so. He only arched an eyebrow, and muttered, "Oh, about the surveillance thing?" That, of course, piqued my interest tantalizingly, but I resisted questioning him for fear of exposing the holes in my own story. Instead, I filed it away as something to bring up with her. "Yeah," I answered cagily.

"Why doesn't she want us to know she's here?"

I stroked the hot, silky skin of his back while we whispered. "I just don't know her very well at all,

Alvaro. When I got back from Santiago, she called me out of the blue, asked me this favor. I said yes. Is she typically…strange?'

He stilled his angular face for a moment, considering whether to answer frankly. "Yeah, she's crazy."

Cheeks glowing as if I had gone running, I returned to find her intent on some ridiculous needlepoint tableau of a meadow. For lack of a better approach, I trotted out the same guacamole recipe I had used on Alvaro, and set to work on chopping and mushing as I pushed the bonding process into grotesque corners of human relations it never intended to go. Plying her with "good" tequila (What do I know? It was golden and cost more than the other labels.) and a gently relentless barrage of questions, I nudged her toward spilling her entire account of how she came to own surveillance equipment, plant it in my home, figure out what to do with it, and do it. I even benefited from reports of her spiritual hand-wringing and moral soul-searching. She didn't ask me if I was recording her testimony at the moment, so I didn't have to lie. [That night's DVD, supplemented by the following week's installments, provided me with the source material for writing the descriptions of her independent actions in the preceding pages.] Hers was a tedious, yet gripping story. It's not often that one gets to hear one's own undoing narrated, especially outside a court of law. Remember, we were in socks in my living room; I poured the drinks. Before turning in, we yawningly resolved to start work the next morning.

Sleep twisted around my neck like a dark noose—then nothing.

Were there a less hopeful word for morning than "morning", I would use it here, but language fails me. Like a servant in a quilted silk bathrobe, I prepared a pot of coffee, carafe of hot milk, pile of croissants, and jar of marmalade on a tray. I let her stuff her sugar-rotted mouth undisturbed for a few minutes, while I sipped coffee through a clenched jaw. After judging her to be fuelled, I sat at the deadly monolith that used to be my meek little desk, drumming my nails against the lucite. "Ok, Luz-divina. Last time you asked for twenty thousand. This time, it'll be a hundred thousand. Fifty for you, the same for me." She nodded, still chewing. I set up the e-mail screen, and told her, "You go ahead. It needs to read the same. I've printed out their names and addresses, in case you forgot them." I vacated the chair, and she thudded into it. Squinting at the paper list, and typing with the excruciating care of an arthritic, or an illiterate, she wrote the following form letter:

```
Dear _____,
```

This is the FINAL letter from me. I
have still many discs. If you don't
want me to send copies to your
family and office, you'll send
US$100,000 to the same bank account.
You can use 72 hours. After that, I
send. I NEVER contact you again.

Salutations,
Ximena

    She showed it to me for approval. "Fine. That's
fine. Let me do the rest." I couldn't bear to sit
through her halting process of copying all the names
and addresses. Figuring she had forgotten to, in her
nervousness at being watched, I selected her text and
converted to Courier. Clicking "send" felt like firing
a silenced handgun five times in a row. I had one
bullet left in the chamber, assuming the metaphor left
room for six, like in films. She spent the whole day
listening to the radio and needlepointing, while I
caught up on some back reading. The journals were
talking a lot about digitization of archives, and I
knew just what they meant. The Society had a way
to go before it could hope to compare to its sister
institutions in Europe, what with their superior
funding.
    Then a disturbing e-mail came to dissolve
entirely my already fraying nerves. It was my boss,

apologizing for disturbing me during my no doubt challenging time in Chile, but there was a problem. A certain volume, *The Paradise Garden Murals of Malinalco: utopia and empire in sixteenth-century Mexico,* out-of-print, of course, like most of our holdings, which had been entrusted to my care, seemed to be missing. Needless to say, it couldn't actually be missing, (González-Feinmann seemed on the verge of putting this bit in bold face, but then resisted), but my temporary replacement could not locate it. Ordinarily, this kind of thing would be far from urgent—ha ha ha—but the book was needed right away for a loan to a university. He would appreciate the swiftest response I could muster from my outpost.

My blood froze, slush clogging my veins. Oh, no. What had I been thinking? Stealing and then making a gift of a purloined item was so *not me* that I could scarcely recall, let alone understand, doing it. I must have been in some sort of fugue state when I made that regrettable choice. Neither for the first nor last time, I felt Luz-d's corrosive influence on my character like a creeping skin fungus. I longed to scrape it off, but it would require slow, careful treatment.

I ran through my options mentally, but my mind was an ice-encrusted highway with too many unmarked exits, and no enforced speed limit. I

couldn't think—especially not with that whale
beached in my living room. I needed to put it down
on paper. Rifling through my carry-on for my little
notebook—discarding boarding passes and crumpled
tissues along the way—I breathed deeply, vainly
trying to feel in control.

The truth: that I made a gift of the
book to someone who helped me in a
time of need, someone who would
genuinely appreciate it, as his
ancestors may have actually
commissioned those murals.
The truth would probably have a
certain nobility for González-
Feinmann, but to tell him that, I'd
have to tell him that I was in
Mexico, not Chile, and look like a
liar. (Too damaging.)
The lies: 1. It was stolen off my
desk at the Society. (Too
implausible.)
2. It was stolen out of my hotel
room in Santiago de Chile. (Admits
I improperly borrowed it.)
3. I left it on the airplane,
groggy with sleeping aids. (Still
admits I improperly borrowed it.)
4. I have no idea. (Complete
bafflement.)

I read and re-read my list until it started to look less like English and more of a detached novelty, like a Mayan codex, that had no bearing on my life. I shimmied into my bathing suit, told Lulu to make herself at home, and rode the elevator to Pool level. It was mercifully empty, waiting for me, placid and sterile as the womb. Lap after lap, I reconsidered my choices, which all clearly sucked. There would be no way to emerge with my credibility unscathed. The very best I could do would be to not incriminate myself directly, but at least leave my worst indiscretions to the imagination. I would abandon myself to Fate. Erupting out of the water, I chose Number Four, deniability, plausible or not.

I evicted Lulu, who was bidding on some crap in an online auction, from my plastic throne, and composed an e-mail to my boss, from Chile, indicating that I hadn't the foggiest idea as to the whereabouts of the book. I had left a pile of to-be-cataloged materials on my desk—beyond that, I couldn't say. I hinted that my replacement should have a clearer idea, as she—I assumed her to be female, given the low wage to education ratio—was there in my seat. Sending it, I had the ominous sensation that always accompanies wrongdoing. My stomach flipped.

*Vuelve a mirar el castigo/ sin venganza. No es
tomarla/ el castigar la justicia.*

Look again upon the punishment without revenge.
Justice's punishing is not taking revenge.
TRANSLATION MINE

Another endless night passed with my servant in
the cloying role of guest. A inexplicably chatty
dinner (she was in a buoyant mood over the incoming
wealth, I guess), then interminable hot cocoas, during
which she narrated the ceaseless humiliations she had
experienced during years of housecleaning: shit
caked between bathroom tiles, health-destroying
fungi in long-neglected microwave-safe containers,
sink drains clogged with vomit, dandruffy hair
brushes, piss-sticky floors. "You were the cleanest
and best house I ever had," she praised me.

Breakfast the following morning was the most
awkward I've had since the first time that
overgroomed shark "Uncle" Kyle was allowed to
sleep over with Aunt Suzie. Then, I had gritted my
teeth and clanked porcelain with exaggerated
sullenness. This time, I had to smile encouragingly at
my tormentor, as I still needed several favors.
Holding the sugar jar open for her pleasure like a
lifted skirt on a child whore, I reminded her, "We
ought to log on to the bank account, to see if anyone

has responded yet." I held my breath for a moment, wondering if she would take umbrage at the "we", or if she would feel hideously strange about the fact that only one of us had the password. Ignoring the silver tongs, and grabbing two sugar cubes with her bare hands, she smiled at me with an idiotic innocence that seemed to be demanding a strike across the face-- and recall that I'm normally distanced from any violent urges. She was special. "Yes, Ximena, I will see." Her entitlement was too much. So irritated my bowels were loosening, I had to step out onto the terrace to grapple with my composure. Up until that point, I had been considering many different ways to defraud her of the money, but then, with gradual swiftness, like a solar eclipse, my mind darkened, and I knew that worse things than a reversion to poverty would have to befall her. Unclenching my fists, I felt relieved and reborn at the same time, also lightheaded. It wasn't me who had decided this, but Fate. Staring into the river, I stopped worrying. A higher power was in control now; I was nothing but the lissome doll who would help along justice. The sky looked limitless with promise, blue beyond reason. You could even say I was happy.

Refreshed, I received the news that all but Pedro had paid up already. *Transfers pending*, parroted Luz-d, like an infant imitating speech. Not bad, it was a huge sum. I had to wonder if Pedro was just

lagging, or had decided not to cooperate. I would
give him a few days before I leapt to conclusions.
She had logged out, and left the *Thank you for
banking with us* screen up to taunt and insult me.
Silently, I closed the windows, drew the blinds, and
safety locked the door. My heart pounded, but it felt
good. "Luz-divina," I asked sweetly, "would you go
back to the computer and show me how to set up my
own account? That way, you can transfer my half
without problems." From where she stood in the
kitchen, chopping vegetables for a meal that was
never to be, she obediently lumbered to my
transparent chair, and set to work typing with two
fingers. I entered the mirrored sanctuary of my
closet, pausing to look into my own eyes, to see
myself for one last time as I was. I mentally recorded
the image, filing it away for a future I couldn't
imagine. Fondly rubbing the smooth surfaces of my
latex garments, I slipped out of my shoes and sunk
barefoot into the carpet. Its soft pile filled the spaces
between my toes, comforting me like a tiny embrace.
I opened one special drawer and calmly removed the
red rubber ball gag, the riding crop, the padded wrist
and ankle cuffs, and the bar that connected the two.
I set them in a neat pile on the floor. Hesitating with
the severe finality of my gesture, I reached to the
back right-hand corner of the drawer, to stroke the
grey velvet pouch I never opened. Yanking it out by

its grey satin drawstring, I silently held it, with the light, cupping grip of a doctor's hand on a scrotum sac. This was the only remaining vestige of Mr. Amsterdam, as I had long ago spent everything he'd paid me, and certainly had no photographs or letters from our relation. Just a smattering of excessively vivid memories of his extreme, impressively committed sadism connected his stun gun to its provenance. He had relocated to the Maldives for work, and had never come to collect his favorite prop. There the little weapon had sat, in an unseen corner of my special drawer, a fragrant sachet, permeating all the drawer's contents with its essence, over the course of uncounted nights, from apartment to new apartment. I unleashed it into my palm, where its ergonomics felt immediately right. The black plastic soothed my nervously sweating palm. A new battery lay smugly at the bottom of the pouch—Mr. Amsterdam had been far too painstaking to ever risk the humiliation of a dead battery. I broke it out of its wrapper, and gingerly put it in. Though I had never used the stunner before, I knew all too well how it worked. I would never forget the crackling oblivion it imparted to the recipient of its charms. It was like one's brain had been replaced by pain for an instant. It hurt purer than anything else I'd known. I pressed the trigger, careful to keep the arc zone away from myself. It worked. Oh, it worked.

I set it down on top of the pile of objects, and gathered them in my arms. As if in a trance, I walked, still barefoot, to the square of floor directly behind the raptly computing monster at my desk. In a grotesque choreography of perfect efficiency, I did something quite unlike myself: zapping her with electricity in the back of the neck, I took advantage of her stunned, momentary paralysis to shove the gag into her slack drooling mouth, and fasten it. As she came to, I zapped her again, and methodically cuffed her hands behind her back, repeating the process until her ankles were bound, connected to her wrists behind the chair. I didn't pause to reflect until she was fully subdued. When I did, I saw my whole life and identity in ashed ruins; I couldn't recognize my actions. Soaked in urine, and dripping saliva, Luzdivina looked terrible. A beautifully formed woman bound is one thing—this was quite another. Her eyes bulged with panic, while her hips lamely tried to gyrate free. Far from pornographic, the scene was pathetic. But remember, Reader, she did it to herself.

"I'm sorry about this," I told her, "Truly sorry, but you know what? *You* never apologized to *me* for what you did." She bulged her eyes at me again. "And you should have." My apartment was a shambles. I'd never seen it so filthy before, and that disturbed me. I picked up the pace of my monologue, so as to get this unpalatable business

over with. "Luz-divina, I'm not going to hurt you"—
I lied—"If you cooperate with me, you can get up
and leave here in good form. If you don't, that's a
problem." I zapped her again to underscore what I
meant by *problem*.

Inside her mind, scenarios were being crafted
and pulled apart like magnet shavings in psychedelic
patterns. She relived each of her decisions, hurtling
violently through time, until she arrived at the
hideous present moment. Did she relate her
predicament to the performances she'd viewed on the
surveillance records? We'll never know. I'd never
wanted to hurt another living being. I'd spent my life
recycling the blinding, stylized pain leveled against
me into kindness and delicacy. Mine was a world of
books, paintings, custom-made lingerie, wood-
paneled libraries lit by warm chandeliers, walks
along the river bank with my imperturbably elegant
canine pet. The indescribable vulgarity of the torture
scene affected me.

Let me pause this DVD chapter to return to the
night before. I should have mentioned that in my
insomniac desperation, I had made a pot of *chili con
carne* from scratch, using grass-fed fed beef and
organic beans. While Lulu slumbered, I was still
crafting ways to ingratiate myself with her, you see.
I had stowed it in the fridge, intending to re-heat it
whenever I wanted to make her feel welcome.

Returning to the terrible action, I rapped the riding crop across her meaty shoulder blade, and recalled the pot of comfort food that sat waiting to be consumed.

After asking her several times for the password to the electronic bank account, and having her shake her head furiously in refusal, I became impatient, and struck her face with the leather crop. Then she signaled that I should remove the shiny red ball gag, and she would tell me. "Luz, I hope you're trustworthy now. If you scream, you'll find yourself much unhappier than now. If you peacefully tell me what I need, I'll untie everything and serve lunch. There's homemade *chili con carne*. Ok?" She nodded forcefully. I gingerly undid the buckle at the back of her neck, careful to keep the stun gun close at hand in case I needed to silence her. But, I didn't. She was well-silenced by the trail of bloody saliva that gushed from her lips when I released her jaw. She stared at me with pure, freezing hatred. "Tell me."

She cleared her throat, gurgled, burped. "Ximena," I thought she said, "but with a J."

"So, J-I-M-E-N-A?"

"Yes." She started crying. I turned the laptop toward me, and still standing, tried to log on to the account. It worked. There before me in soothing tones of white and blue pranced my balance, a long number as lithe and upbeat as a line of chorus girls. I immediately went into my account settings and changed the password to something a little more secure, then turned my attention back to my maid.

"Thank you, you did the right thing finally. Want some lunch?" I left her bound and blubbering, and went into the kitchen, buoyed by my new wealth. My mind raced diligently around the dilemma of how to launder the cash, but I managed to focus on the stew. Rummaging through the fridge, my eye caught on the jar of creamy peanut butter from which I used to sparingly dole out Segismundo's favorite treat. It was still half-full, and I had kept it as a sort of memorial to my best friend. Now fully finished with Luz-d, and re-enraged about my dog, I decided to stir the last of it into the pot. It melted nicely, seeping into the overwhelmingly spicy mixture without a visible trace. When it was piping hot, I served it in bowls and brought them out. I untied her hands so she could feed herself. "Here, eat up. You'll feel better." Utterly defeated, she obeyed. She sat, I stood, and together we gobbled down the delicious dish whose recipe I had gotten from a cooking website. It was tangy and exciting on the tongue.

A minute later, she was dead. It's called anaphylactic shock, and is apparently the greatest fear of allergy sufferers. Segismundo's peanut butter was startlingly efficient, silent, its effect somewhat riveting to behold. I quickly untied the rest of her, uncuffed her ankles, put the props back into their drawer, and massaged her bloated ankles to smooth out the lines left by the padded cuffs. Her wrists were fine, having been liberated earlier.

I dialed 911. They arrived swiftly in a maelstrom of red light. The medics wore blue and were fit and handsome. The shorter of the two declared her dead in a tone both somber and routine. I frantically related how my former maid had asked to stay with me for a couple of days, I had agreed, and we had just sat down to a light lunch when she stopped breathing, starting convulsing and drooling blood, and I called them. Then I wept. Patting my back and stroking my hair, the taller of two asked me to show them her purse. Trembling, I led them to her stuff, repeating confusedly that I knew almost nothing about her, nothing at all. She was just my maid! They loaded her body onto a gurney, covered it with a wool blanket, and we all left together to fill out forms and complete procedures. In the lobby, I sobbingly begged Alvaro to come along. He wept, too, and gripped my hand sweatily. But he declined to get involved, smart man.

When I finally called in to the Society, I stumbled into a concrete barrier of awkwardness. First, González-Feinmann's secretary put me on hold for entire minutes. Then, she got back on herself, uneasily stammering, "Uh, Ximena? Could, could he call you back? He's in a meeting." I could hear her bad teeth and the loneliness in her voice. An hour later, it was him, wriggling and writhing in his invisible chair.

"How was your trip, dear?" He coughed away from the receiver, but it could still be heard. I launched into a detailed fictitious account of my journey, which included *churrasco* sandwiches, long waits in notaries' offices, and Pacific weather fronts. González-Feinmann coughed again. "Did you manage to locate that missing volume?"

"No."

"For us, that's problematic. It places a strain on our fundraising abilities when volumes of note are requested and not provided to our sister institutions. I think you know what I mean." I did. I coughed daintily in response. What could I really say? "Ximena, we've had quite a lot of success with your temporary substitute." A chill shot down my spine.

"You have?"

"Yes," he croaked.

"You mean…" A blast of clarity called up an image in my mind: Pedro Algodón's face. This wasn't strictly about one purloined book. Incensed with the extortion, though not fully sure as to my role in it, Pedro had recalled the special favor of my employment from his old friend. I was being excised like a tumor before I could do any more damage to his family. My book stupidity had removed even my right to righteous self-defense. All I could I do was play along, try to read my lines correctly from a script one could only guess at.

"We think it would be better if you worked in a different capacity for a little while. Just until you resettle."

"Where would I work, Dr. González-Feinmann?"

"Well, Pamela in Audio-Visual Resources is looking for someone to assist her with their project identifying damaged reels. I spoke to her and she would be more than glad to have your help."

I couldn't help laughing, but chomped down on the interior of my cheek to stop it. I tasted tangy blood. "Sir, that work is a bit…young for me, wouldn't you say? The posting didn't even call for a postgraduate degree."

He coughed four times in quick succession. "I'm afraid it's what we have open at the moment. We're not a large outfit, as you know."

"I'm afraid that might not be very gratifying work for me," I said, feeling shards of glass underfoot. I took a deep breath, diving into the part of the drama that had been written most cruelly. "Please accept my resignation. I tender it with deep regret."

Huge sigh of relief on his end. "I see," he breathed. "I'm sorry this had to resolve itself this way. You know, we always deeply appreciated your skills here. You were a tremendous help, and I want you to know that I will write you only the most glowingly satisfied reference letters. This was not all in my control."

"I understand," I assured him, and I did. His top priority was always to maintain a bubble of peace around himself. He couldn't tolerate even a hint of tension with friends or colleagues. I only wondered which lie Pedro had told him, though I had no doubt that it was less outlandish than the truth. "I learned a lot here, and for that I'm grateful. Please accept my apology for the lost book, and please do write me a reference letter that I can start using right away." His cough had disappeared, replaced by a wistful breath.

Now jobless, but far from penniless, I experienced a burst of energy that was like rebirth. Had I stopped to analyze my elation, I would have found within myself the primordial human joy that comes from having slain one's adversary. I had killed, and come out unscathed. However, I wasn't quite ready to look that hard at what I'd done. It was too awful, too out of character, way too aggressor and not nearly enough victim to suit my image of myself. I would push it aside and forge ahead with my plan for survival.

Cash, I realized, is a lot like good reading material. You can never have too much back-up. The comfort of the nest egg Luz-d had graciously set up for me begged to be increased. I would think about it over a bottle of Rioja.

Come to think of it, why drink alone? Even if I was out of business, I could still use some male companionship. So, I called Alvaro—yes, her cousin—no, I didn't feel particularly villainous—and invited him to join me. We were both grief-stricken, both sheepish on account of having denied any connection to her to the authorities. He wasn't technically her cousin, anyway, and she wasn't technically Rosalba, anyway, and I was technically just a housecleaning client, so it had made sense to us to leave her body at the morgue. They would do whatever is done with unclaimed bodies. Alvaro was traumatized enough with having had to make the hideous long-distance call to the dusty valley. "I'm thoroughly traumatized," he succinctly reported. He couldn't further worry her family with funeral costs. It was easier just to tell them she was nicely buried in a New York cemetery they would never see. "Dead is dead," was his rationalization, and I liked it.

After draining a glass each and enjoying an hour of head-clearing exertions, the bright side of things began to sneak into focus. I myself had never thought of videorecording my sessions, but now that I had seen them, I could see that they had real aesthetic merit. Well-lit and simply composed, a connoisseur would get intense pleasure from viewing them, I was sure. I feigned sleepiness, Alvaro departed, and I got to work. It felt good, cleansing, to immerse myself in research once again. Hours and three yogurts later, I had identified a distribution entity in the Netherlands that would be serious enough to acquire my archive. A sort of video club, they required that a signed legal agreement be faxed to an office in Leiden before one could even begin paying rather substantial dues.

And so, the next two weeks became an inner vision quest and porn marathon, both, during which I put my years of library service to good use. The dearly departed had kindly ordered the Ximena Show episodes chronologically, so I only had to tag them (Nipple Torture, Rope Burns, Crying, and the like), and then painstakingly mosaicize the men's faces into unrecognizability. This last task took forever, but wasn't unpleasant—it felt good to blur out their distinctive features into a throbbing mass of anonymous pixels. It was like physics, or art restoration, an exploration of boundaries and meaning. Having no parents to embarrass meant I would leave my own face sharp and clear as a recess bell. I was free.

After a couple of work-intensive days, I needed to get out, interface a little. So, I called Lindsay with the news that I was back from Chile, and suggested we grab a bite. She was looking very much the wilted daisy when I spotted her in a window booth overlooking Second Avenue, but deliberately perked up when I sat down across from her. Sporting a CIAO, BELLA ROMA tee, the poor thing was trying to maintain a veneer of happiness. Lining up my pro-biotic capsules along the bottom edge of my water glass, I asked her to tell me all about it. I hoped her tale would be long and involved, so there'd be no time left to grill me about Santiago, my dead parents, and the winter-in-summer/ summer-in-winter stuff.

Long and involved it was: Apparently unable to resist the inexorable pull toward intra-office dalliance, optimistic Linz had been seeing a nearby human rights lawyer in secret, *but only because it looks bad to fraternize.* She would meet him at his apartment, an orderly, if drab outfit on Third Avenue, for hastily consumed dinners followed by what she experienced as passionate sex. This continued for several weeks, during which time, she *felt herself falling in love*, and began harboring hopes that they could start doing *couple things* like going running along the river and getting drinks in bars. Then one day, while scouring the downtown vintage shops for European t-shirt acquisitions, she spotted him striding down the avenue *with his doppelganger at his heels*. Whoa, wait, I had to stop her there.

"What does it mean, 'his doppelganger at his heels'?"

Lindsay eyes flashed with rage. "Thank you for asking. Indeed, what is a man doing with his exact double?"

"A twin brother?"

"Precisely," she said, getting even more inexplicably incensed.

"So…?"

"So, when we first met, when I asked him if he had any siblings, he said no."

"You sure, Linz?"

"Sure I'm sure. He even described himself as 'an only child'."

"He used the phrase 'only child'?"

"Yeah, X. More than once."

The rest of the story unrolled like as a sad scroll as my friend, my only friend recounted the step-by-step discovery of the deflating news that she actually had been sleeping with not one, but two men, both of them married, with—believe it or not—a set of twins each. Identical twins show up in some families in high frequency clusters like that. A gene, apparently. Much to her chagrin, Lindsay had not even been the only butt of this particular practical joke: several consecutive days of staking out his "apartment" revealed it to be a well-trafficked pied-à-terre rented for just such a sordid purpose.

Friendships between adult women, I found out during my crash course with Linz, are judged by the quality of the commiseration. I performed outrage and shock and devastation, my face contorting beyond its customarily placid proportions, yet I was distracted by a tone of thought that had recently come to color my mind, and would only increase over time. I emphatically did not want to tell Lindsay about my having been fired from the Society. It wasn't, as you might be guessing, owing to shame, but to a far more diaphanous feeling—I didn't want to be there anymore. Whatever thread had held me dangling from the edge of New York City had suddenly snapped, and I couldn't stomach the inevitable career counseling that would follow such an admission. The city that had formerly held me entranced now seemed like nothing more than a heap of bills to pay, a holding pen for moonlighting double-timers. As I grimaced and coo'd with Lindsay, I re-watched my newly edited video archive in my mind, at 32x speed and with the sound off, and I paused it at a moment of bright transcendence, and I made that freeze frame into a still, and I burnt that still into a corner of my peripheral vision, where it could be seen constantly, but comprehended never, and I vowed to start everything over, reboot my reality as many times as it would take to live forever inside that sunlit space. I would be new. I interrupted her, "Linz, when I was in Chile, I decided to relocate there. You're welcome to visit as soon as I get a place, but until then, I won't be around much." Never mind that I had never actually been there, I now knew that I would be living off Luz-divina's contributions in my father's homeland. It felt correct. It felt new.

Gave notice to The Cloister's rental office today. They said that breaking the lease would be no problem, as there is already a waiting list of waiting young women who would like to move in next month. Decided not to buy back the tapestry. It's too old.

How did I come to find myself among the feminine incarcerated? Has it taken this long to circle round to the question? Was justice, that hammy star of the Spanish Golden age stage, served? Of course not. Let's remember that in the New World colonies, the slaves can only slave so well because they are invisible. One more, one less, one comes, one goes, another one slips past the sentry guards to replace one whom the dark bird of death has carried away—or something to that effect. No, I was never arrested in connection with L-divina's demise.

Instead, I found myself longing to plug the gaping holes left in my life by the Society, the Cloister, and Lindsay respectively. (She flipped out, claiming *abandonment issues* when she heard, that day at the diner, that I was leaving. She found *goodbyes really hard*, and decided she would rather be angry than sad when I took off.) I called the art dealer Paul Lewis again, on the pretext of some manuscript sale inquiries, and gave him the chance to invite me out for dinner. Then, over florette salads, (he turned out to be the rare hetero male anorexic—I liked it) he told me all about the non-profit work he had gotten into as an effort to balance and *humanize* himself. He said *humanize* with an arched eyebrow that either was meant to underscore or undermine the meaning of the word; I never did get to know him well enough to know which. His group, **art**onthe**inside**, commissioned and curated prisoners' art works, and then represented them, pro bono, to collectors. "This kind of thing is done a lot, the whole prisoner art scene, but the way we're different is that we never publicize or exploit the fact that these artists are behind bars. Our collectors never even know they ever bought prison art. We frame them simply as hot young artists who happen to be extremely shy and opening-phobic. And we get them top dollar."

"But can they spend the money?"

"Not at the moment, no, but we're not talking about lifers here. So, it's held in escrow until release. Some of them have asked me to invest it for them in the interim, so I do."

"What kind of investment?"

"Whatever they request. Usually mutual funds? Sometimes specific things like emerging markets?"

"Prisoners have specifically requested emerging markets?"

"Ximena, a murderer isn't necessarily an idiot."

I blushed, then blushed again in a second wave, realizing. Some murderers are actually very cultivated young ladies.

A week passed, and Paul Lewis invited me out for salads again. I nibbled on dandelion greens; he stuffed them into his mouth with an aggressive flourish. I narrated a re-edited version of reality that concluded in my quitting my job and my apartment out of a growing distaste for the consumer frenzy and cultural vacuity of New York. I painted a portrait of a woman on a vision quest to reconnect with her ancestral heritage in the Switzerland of South America. He nodded knowingly; admiration glinted off his eyeglass lenses like rays of a benevolent sun. Then he cut to the point. "I guess it's pretty cheap to live down there, huh?"

"Well, Paul, it depends how you look at it. Compared to some of its riots-in-the-streets, narco-militia neighbors, it's expensive. But yes, for a rooftop-swimming-pool kind of society, it's dirt." I brushed his knee with my ankle.

His knee tensed with anticipation, if you can picture that, and he told me, "I wouldn't try to get you to cancel your plans…but a postponement of dreams only makes their realization sweeter." That was when he told me about a minimum security lady prison with which he worked that was looking for an Interim Librarian until they hired someone permanent. The last one had had to resign with no notice after having been discovered trading prescription diet pills to young inmates for sexual favors. According to Paul, a headhunter was already scouring the land for possible candidates, so the whole job would not last more than a couple of months. Seeing as how the *campus*, as they called it, was in a leafy community North-west of the city, I would be staying rent-free in the facilities.

"In a cell?" I joked. (See, even double spontaneous orphans can joke sometimes.)

"They don't call them cells, but yeah, sort of? They don't have special librarian housing? So, it would be regular campus housing? Nights off, you're always welcome in my home." The bullet can never stall in its trajectory.

The formality of the interview behind me, I told the warden with the corporate pastel pantsuits and defeated eyes that I could start in a week's time. She called herself Pam and consulted her handheld frequently. Pam thanked me and assured me that my experience at the facility would be *enriching* and *eye-opening*.

It took a single day to place what few possessions I still had in Paul Lewis' art warehouse. Then I was on the red eye to Santiago, sharing the air in my lungs with hordes of skiing enthusiasts who lacked the patience to wait for the season to catch up with their passions. Would you believe I felt a little nostalgic for my one plane journey with L-divina? I did. I almost sort of missed the dog killer, and my eyes moistened as I pictured her jowly face and elephantine gait. Recalling the champagne she'd brought me from First Class, I flagged a hookerish stewardess and ordered one, reveling in the width of my First Class berth. Luz-d had done much to help me afford the more delicate conveniences.

As I lay cocooned in buttery beige airline socks, matching sleep mask, and foam earplugs, my mind wandered to the far corners of memory. Sensory deprivation is so good for that. Again and again, I replayed my maid's death, its foaming, squirming horror, and I felt enraged. I tossed and turned in my flattened seat, fuming at the unfairness of it all. By what quirk of Destiny was I always placed in close proximity to atrocity? Why did Tragedy stalk me? Why did Sadness have to be my life-long friend? I dove back into my cold mental swimming pool to relax. After a few dozen thought-laps, my body became limp and my mind sank like a stone, drifting, drifting toward the impossible mosaic at the bottom.

A second later, I was disembarking into a clear, mild winter day, picking up my bag from among the bundled snowboards on the conveyor belt, and fastening my taxi seat belt with a satisfying click. We sped toward the Capital. On both sides of the road, space spread out absolutely, unhindered: monotonously well-ordered vineyards, signposted with multi-national wine brand names, stretched like nets over the earth. Figures in shiny yellow rubber suits and helmets sprayed poison in broad strokes over the vines. It didn't feel like the Chile I'd imagined, but like a blank zone that had been earmarked for grapes. Intermittently, a blossoming plum tree would appear in front of a corrugated tin roofed shack, then disappear again into the vineyards like an optical illusion. I was more alone than I'd ever been, strangely looking forward to the structure of the prison, but sure that this was where I wanted to live. I would stay alone until I'd purged New York from my veins. I would stay alone until I could look

at a jar of peanut butter without my bowels
loosening.

Santiago de Chile. A sedate city where the miserably poor build Modernist condos for the spectacularly wealthy. Blue skies that mock their own pollutants with brilliance. The jagged peaks of the Andes are visible from every spot in the city except the underground metro. There, blond men in spread collars type furiously on laptops. Dark teenagers sulk in loose clothes. The real estate agent was efficient and lean. We looked at eleven apartments in a single day, stopping only twice. Once for coffee, once for greasy meat sandwiches. I think she was a little amazed at my decisiveness. I paid in full for the third thing we saw, a two-bedroom unit in El Golf, a manicured neighborhood free of street urchins.

That was a cinch. The unlikely named Banco
Paris single-handedly accepted my huge transfer
from Lulu's electronic account and cut a real-world
check for the real estate. So far, it didn't look like I
would be hassled about the cash lump that was both
my burden and my freedom. I was just another guilty
murderer spending good money in Chile.

However, I rehearsed, again and again, my
reaction in front of the mirror if I were ever
questioned by any authorities. I was a victim of
identity theft by a crooked maid.   I thought I had
straightened it all out, but still now (the eternal now,
whenever trouble comes up is now) it was hard to
separate out all the dirty threads, impossible to return
my finances to the pristine state they were in before
she came sweeping (and mopping) into my life.
She's dead now, so it's hard to get answers.

I liked the soothing tones of the Banco Paris
branches. They were decked out in a cheery,
detergent aquamarine that promised a future purged
of all past. Banking there felt like an injection of
pool chlorine into my veins, especially when they
referred to me in the third person as La Ximena.
They gave me some more of my own freshly
laundered cash to spend on renovations to my new
home: eggshell walls, checkerboard floors, and a six-
head shower (one can never be too clean) were set in
motion before I left for what I had affectionately

come to think of as my *prison term*. Prices being so reasonable, I went ahead and arranged for the contractors to turn the second bedroom into a super-closet, where I would warehouse all the finery that had, I believe, driven Lulu a little mad. The power of the sartorial over fat women can never be overstated. I could only demurely shake my head when asked if I was sure I wouldn't rather keep it as a maid's room.

And so I retraced my air steps to JFK, savoring each exploding champagne bubble on my tongue like so many bullets in the war against misery. Again, I played the footage of my parents diving into the Chilean earth at its highest, sharpest point. Behind my closed eyelids, their stomachs flipped as they dropped from the sky into an impromptu cremation. (I can confide in you now that you've read this far: My secret faith has always been the belief that one or both of them could think only of me in those last frames.) I was already scared of my new life before knowing what shape it would take. A cog in the wheel of the destiny machine is all each of us will ever be, sure, but it's rare to feel that truth burning in the pit of your stomach as it did in mine. The clouds outside the windows seemed to have been placed there by the hand of a G-d who wanted to obscure my vision, to dazzle and confound me first, before showing me the light.

I've been here now two weeks—just six more to go.

The inmates tend to fall into one of two basic categories: the Ximena's and the Luz-divina's. A handful of them are neither, but they tend to have committed crimes of passion, which don't really interest me at the moment, since they don't tell me anything about my maid's inner life. I like chatting with the Luz-divina's who methodically plotted out every last detail of some mechanistic plot designed to right the wrongs handed down by Fate. The last paragraph of their stories always retracts this attitude, resigning the teller to her destiny, almost beatifically accepting Reality's will. They make for helpful kitchen assistants and seamstresses.

It's charming, too, in an eerie way, to chat with the Ximena's, thwarted beauties whose commitment to utter perfection landed them in deep trouble. The lot of them are double spontaneous orphans in one way or another, variations on the theme. Like looking into a warped mirror, one scratched and clouded with overuse and neglect, they show me the path I would've had no choice but to take had Luck abandoned me in those, my most crucial hours. I let them help me in the Library.

I'm hoping to use these weeks in such spare surroundings to record this story in my small orderly notebook, then be done with it, place it in a corner of my well-lit, tidily arranged closet, next to the stun gun. May they both gather dust.

Look! An unflinching hand, merciless, iron-like,
crushes her infidel will like a wounded sparrow
caught underboot…a celestial light leaks out from
between sooty clouds. She weeps!

Anonymous
from *Treasures of the Golden Age*
TRANSLATION MINE
ITALICS MINE

THE PLEASURE ALL MINE

APPENDIX 1

xx/ xx/ 2007

My treasure,
Yes, I still call you that. Are you
surprised?

You must certainly be surprised to
receive a letter from me at your new
address. How do you suppose I came
upon it? Not by scanning the X's of
the Santiago public phone directory,
to be sure. No, it was stranger
than that—

One recent day, a fair-haired young
employee bumped into me rather
conspicuously in the corridor. As
she excused herself, she muttered,
Check your left pocket. Bizarre,
like something out of a spy film.
Well, I checked and found a note
that read, *Meet me at the mezzanine
bar at Grand Central Terminal at 7
tonight. I know where she is now*.
I had no doubt to which *she* she was
referring. So, I was nearly fed up
nursing a Scotch on the rocks when,
at 7:23, the same blonde appeared
wearing a shirt that read *Besitos
Infinitos*. A message from you, I

guessed. Or just some new youth
trend? Who knows?

She sat with me and, after a few
minutes of generic pleasantries, she
handed me this South American street
address on a slip of paper. No
name, just the address. As she got
up to leave, I asked her why she
didn't just slip *that* note into my
pocket to begin with. She smiled,
and at that moment, she looked
bewitching for the first time since
I'd seen her. She said that you had
no idea she had contacted me— you
might even be angry with her, but
she didn't care. She only knew that
I had dropped you (her word, not
mine: *dropped*), and that you missed
me, and had possibly even fled the
country solely because of this. She
added that she needed to *experience
me herself.* (Well, probably not.
Anyway,) I assured her that I would
never tell you from whence I learned
your whereabouts. Is it treachery
that I am now? Anyhow, it was quite
clear to me that this so-called *best
friend* knew little to nothing about
you or our situation. Or our
misunderstanding. I'm hoping you'll
explain it to me sometime. You've

only become more mysterious over
time.

I haven't visited Chile since it was
the cause célèbre of the continent
years ago, but for you I would re-
enter that shard of banality that
mars the American map. I'm a bit
surprised at you. I wouldn't have
pictured you making yourself at home
in such a bland and aspirational
capital of the petit-bourgeoisie,
but then again, I do understand the
power of creation myths. I hate to
repeat myself, but I must: What did
happen? Who, or what, came between
us? How were you taken from me?

A word from you, a nod, and I'm
there.
P.

APPENDIX 2

xx/ xx/ 2007

Dearest Pedro,

If you are reading this, you have met with Alvaro, my friend and agent in New York, and he has successfully passed on to you this thick envelope that I dared not mail to your home or office. You can trust him.

Enclosed you'll find the answers to all your questions. Please refrain from scanning or duplicating this manuscript in any way. Simply return it to me, via Express Post, after you've read it. If you still want to see me, you may do so.

We already know that you can destroy me and I can destroy you and you can destroy me. Let's let those facts cancel each other out in perpetuity, so that any thoughts of treachery and vengeance are stripped away, and only the glowing center of what we once had remains.

Yours loyally,

X

AFTERWORD

It is with a heavy heart that I edit these pages, which are comprised of the episodic confession of Jennifer Xaviera Schneider, selections from her journal, and a few of her correspondences.

I knew her as an exemplary librarian and as the close companion of a friend of mine. To say I was shocked to hear of her death is an understatement. It is a matter of heartbreaking regret to acknowledge that her beauty and exuberance were snuffed out by common street thugs, covetous of the diamond earrings that a close Reader will recall were a family heirloom, on a warm Spring evening in Santiago's Parque Forestal. The River Mapocho has run salty tears ever since.

I feel it is incumbent upon me to explain this publication. To do so requires making a few other elucidations first, the comprehension of which requires a temporary suspension of the natural moral outrage of the reader. I hope you'll extend me this courtesy before rushing to judgment.

Why Jennifer/ "Ximena" dubbed my friend from University days "Pedro Algodón" is a mystery to me. This question has compelled me to re-visit the children's classic *Peter Cottontail* more times than I can count, but I have never come to a satisfactory conclusion. In any case, it was Pedro who made these files and papers available to me when it became clear that honoring Jennifer's Last Will with a bound volume would be necessary. While yes, it is self-published, no, it is not *vanity published*, as it is Respect, not Vanity that has engendered the release of these private notes to the public. Jennifer lived for, and at, libraries; she dedicated herself to the institution with a pure heart. It was, I believe, her commitment to such a meagerly compensated trade that pushed her career in the unusual directions demonstrated here. With neither ancestors nor descendants to mourn her senseless passing, it is the bookshelf that will serve as her final resting place.

Perhaps because of her intimacy with loss, young Jennifer had the presence of mind to bequeath her possessions and savings to the Hispanist Society in the same simply drawn Will that expressed her intention to share this story with the public. I have been asked to frankly address the question of whether Jennifer's gift was contingent on the publication and shelf display of her book. So, let me deal with that succinctly: Yes. That said, it is my belief that the Reader who has, goodness knows how, stumbled upon this text will meet with certain enjoyment of its merits, limited as they are. Though repetitious, and an apologist for wrongdoing, the late Miss Schneider is to be applauded for her clear written style and attention to detail.

A brief word, then, on the editing process. I have taken the following liberties: italicization of foreign words and quoted phrases, formatting, and selection. The latter refers to the large chunks of journal entries that have been omitted for the sake of brevity. It would be conservative to estimate that the volume you now hold would have run to 500 pages had I not held its contents to the strictest narrative standards. One can hardly imagine the tedium of reading through detailed descriptions of all 1,300 or so of "Ximena"'s *sessions*.

Now I shall address as concisely as possible the other question that has stalked me at every stage of the process of realizing Miss Schneider's Will. Did the events described occur as they are presented? Yes and no. Upon notification of Jennifer's demise and receipt of her manuscript, I immediately turned all documentation over to the authorities, who were able to confirm the burial of Mrs. Rosalba García Sanchez, as well as the robust existence of the same person in Malinalco, Estado de México, Mexico. Likewise, I was asked to view certain visual media, courtesy of Van der Wahl, Inc. (Leiden, the Netherlands), for identification purposes, and found them to include Jennifer beyond all doubt. However, there shall be no homicide investigation-- it has been explained to me-- because the victim's family has been satisfied by this memoir as a true confession, and of course, the perpetrator is no longer alive. Death is a boundary that cannot be transgressed even by Justice. That said, the mortal remains of "Luz-divina González Salinas" have never been exhumed for identification purposes, nor has her existence ever been officially confirmed.

Despite assurances from the experts, I must say I remain unconvinced that the mild-mannered, assiduous Jennifer I knew is the "Ximena" of the preceding pages. A young woman blessed with beauty, vigor, and intelligence, she cut a strikingly elegant figure at her oversized desk amidst the stacks here at our Library. I have been unable to adequately conjecture as to the source of the not insubstantial sum of her assets at the time of her passing, so I shall refrain from further guesses. If one can content oneself with the somewhat feeble adage, *the end justifies the means,* then one must try to do just that. In her own way, Miss Schneider has greatly assisted the Hispanist Society in its progress toward modernity with the purchase of new and impressive digital archive equipment.

Needless to say, she must have intended for both projects, the philanthropic and the literary, to come to fruition in the far distant future. Alas, the random brutality of a couple of greedy, inhuman boors brought to harvest this crop at an inconceivably early date. To have to execute such a document so prematurely has acquainted me with an unbearable grief, a hitherto unprecedented capacity for forgiveness, and a bitter grudge against Chance.

Dr. Juan Rodríguez-Fleischman
New York City, June 2008

Born in New York, Hillary Raphael is the author of the novels **I [heart] LORD BUDDHA** and **BACKPACKER**, and a study of butoh dance, **OUTCAST SAMURAI DANCER**, with Donald Richie. Please contact her at **hillaryraphael@futurefiction.co.uk**.

www.ingramcontent.com/pod-product-compliance
Lightning Source LLC
Chambersburg PA
CBHW020557250626
47154CB00004B/1260